Termi

at the

Ghost Train
Murder Mystery

CW00495441

We hope you enjoy the Ghost Train Murder Mystery

at Nast Hyde Halt

Y Mars

Mike x

Author's Foreword

Thank you for buying this book. As you may know, once I heard the story of Mike Izzard's restoration at Nast Hyde Halt, I knew it would fit the bill as something special for my fortieth novel.

Of course, most of this work is from Mike himself and my imagination, with fictional inspiration and twisting of tales. (Such as Frederick Field still residing at the Crossing Keepers Cottage in 1971 when in fact he died in 1954, and Mike being postman in the Nast Hyde area), but I also used a lot of external references to shape the story you are about to read. As such, you will find a References list at the back of this book.

Views expressed in this book are neither my own nor Mike's. Everyone mentioned, apart from Mike and Harvey, are fictional. Address details are also fictional, for reasons of privacy and anonymity. No persons or animals were harmed in the making of this book.

Now that's out of the way, a bit about me! Certainly, being born into a railway family helped drive this book forward. My parents met on the local railway in Inverness, so I am a true railwayman's daughter.

As I dislike flying (can't flap my wings hard enough) and my husband agrees, we took our second honeymoon to Italy with Great Rail Journeys. We made friends with Peter, a man who travelled everywhere with a hardback European rail timetable book, much like a Bradshaw's. Most of our group avoided the 'train nerd' throughout the holiday - but Peter's lugging around of the great tome saved us on the way home.

An unfortunate passenger met his maker during the journey through Germany - the poor man was not one of our group - so, the train had to be stopped while necessary procedures were done. Therefore, we all had to transfer to another train to complete our journey. This threw everything into chaos - the delay made us miss connecting trains.

With nothing due to stop there for hours, a slow local already busy train was stopped out of schedule to pick us all up. Peter, our courier, my husband and myself were forced to stand (or try to!) in the train corridor with our party's luggage as everyone crammed gratefully onto the other train. All of our following travel arrangements had to be rebooked, via a patchy phone signal to head office - and with Peter's book to help sort new connections.

I have lots of railway stories in my repertoire as our family holidays were mostly via the country's rail network - a perk of my parents' jobs was free rail travel. I enjoyed this until I was 18, and even now, when heading home I travel by rail.

The 1988 slogan "Let the Train take the Strain" formed part of a hugely successful advertising campaign for British Rail. Researching The Golden Age of Steam for my book, I have discovered similar campaigns over the years.

One of the things on my bucket list is to journey on a steam train. Preferably on a scenic line where I can take LOTS of photos!

I love the old London Routemaster buses, and since moving 'down south' in 2001, I have managed to hop on many. Also, I love the VW Campervan, or as we called them 'dormobiles'.

While writing this book in our garden, I have worked through intermittent interruptions from planes overhead. Modern equivalents to and from Stansted don't interest me, but the older planes to and from North Weald always do.

I guess I'm just a lover of all things vintage!

Acknowledgements

Mike dedicated the restoration of Nast Hyde Halt to Harvey, his beloved canine companion who never lived to see the project finished.

Everyone who has lost their pet will know that they aren't just an animal, they are much more than that - they are a real member of the family. Sometimes they are our only welcoming party upon returning home. Sometimes they are our saving grace, tuning into our moods and helping us get through the times of sadness. Sometimes muddy pawprints on a recently washed floor drive us to distraction - but we'd never have it any other way.

They mean far more to us than a four (or three!) legged friend. I'm relieved there is now a law making pet theft illegal (as of September 2021) - about time too!

A note of thanks to the people who helped me along the way with the writing of this epic tale. Mike, of course; Fred Field's grandson, Roy; my ghostly expert Trudie; my Uncle David; my protege turned editorial adviser, Steve; a mutual friend, Sacha; my right hand woman, Jo; and the advanced readers who helped shape the book.

Special mention to Callum Willcox of Peco.

Yvonne

Special Dedication

This book is dedicated to the memory of
Ethel Violet Mason, who died aged 18 upon the Hatfield to St. Albans
branch line Railway in 1929 at Nast Hyde.
Gone but never forgotten.

Railway History

In the 1840s as the railways grew, they were viewed in fear by a host of long-established trades, from coachbuilders to innkeepers.

When steam engines took over from horses, most stablehands and wagon owners were out of a livelihood virtually overnight. The few stagecoaches that were able to adapt, did so by altering their routes to serve advancing railheads, or provide cross country feeder services.

To do this, some stagecoaches were loaded onto flat wagons attached to trains, where new horses would haul the unloaded coach to its final destination. This saved hours of travelling - up to 5 hours in some cases!

Feeder services were used when it was learned that if a station name had 'road' in it, this meant that they were not near the name on the station sign. The distance between the station and the town could be many miles!

However, the arrival of steam train transport was not all good. Accidental fires could be started by stray sparks to land along the line, wooded areas or any flammable items. Coupled with the high numbers of accidents and deaths associated with working with these giants of iron and hissing steam, many dangers came with the railways.

Soot and dirt on the exposed engine footplate left many drivers and firemen in poor health for their retirement. In the event of an accident, it was these poor unfortunate souls who suffered the most.

Still, it was easy to see why in 1844, Britain was overcome by Railway Mania. The period of 1838-1843 saw many plans for increases in the rail network across the country, although not all of them came to fruition and as a result, many investors lost their money.

An interesting side note is that the railways affected everyone, whether you used them or not. Railway time was the name given to the standardised time arrangement applied in November 1840 by the Great Western Railway[1] (GWR) in England. It was taken up by all of the British railway companies over the seven years that followed, although it was only in 1880 that the government legislated a single time zone for the whole country.

All station clocks and train schedules used London Time, otherwise known as Greenwich Mean Time (GMT). Railway time overcame the confusion caused by non-uniform time in each town and station stop along the railway network. As differences could be up to twenty minutes, by standardising time dangerous incidents due to increased traffic on the lines were also reduced.

Usually, journeys between the larger cities and towns could take many hours or even days, therefore such differences in time could be easily adjusted en route - but with the arrival of the railways, things had to change.

Invention of the electric telegraph meant time signals from Greenwich could be sent through wires alongside railway lines across Britain, and by 1855, 98% of towns and cities had switched to standardised time.

Rail networks in North America (1850s), India (around 1860) and in Europe prompted the standard time introduction, influenced by geography, industrial development and political governance.

Railway travellers found themselves utterly confused by the different times of towns and cities, thus printed timetables for each railway company were required, ergo the birth of the Bradshaw's Guide. These were a series of railway timetables and travel guidebooks, initially produced in 1839 to aid travel over the ever-expanding rail network by detailing each company's timetables.

However, with the amalgamation of more than a hundred railway companies into the Big Four from 1923 onwards, they weren't as necessary. Bradshaw's also had publications for Continental Europe, Australia and New Zealand.

---

1.   https://en.wikipedia.org/wiki/Great_Western_Railway

TERMINATION AT THE HALT, GHOST TRAIN MURDER MYSTERY

The guidebook became famous in recent times as a sidekick to Michael Portillo's 'Great British Railway Journeys' TV series - and onto the 'Great Continental Railway Journeys' TV series. Mike and Michael Portillo met at a special 'Audience With...' night in St. Albans, where Michael congratulated him on his work at Nast Hyde Halt!

Prelude

An important decision was being made by Hatfield Town's Order of the Elite, the secret society of the area (much like the historic Freemasons).

Each of the 1971 Apprentice candidates all stood equal chances: each could represent the way of life of the Order successfully; each had passed the necessary tests to get this far. Each young man had qualities that the Order would find useful and each was in a trade that would conceal the ways of the Order without interrupting society business.

Many aspiring members had failed to get this far. Over the years, appointees who didn't make the annual qualification for continuing membership had moved away from the area, or in war time joined up to leave their old lives behind. Some disappeared...

Nigel Marquis denoted himself regularly as the best candidate for this year's Apprentice. Inheriting his family's bakery in the centre of Hatfield town at the age of 17, after a house fire wiped out his entire family - parents, siblings and pets - life gave Nigel a bitterness. His angst-ridden nature became stubborn and aggressive over the following years. With no distractions by way of family or lovers, his private business remained so; that looked set to continue for a long time. He was best placed to keep an eye on the town and its people.

Those high up in the Order decreed that Nigel was their man. A self-sufficient and successful young business man with no emotional ties would suit their purposes well.

**

Kneeling as he was bade before the men of the Order, Nigel brought their 'names' into his mind. Usually the Apprentice called the higher ranking members 'Sir', but it would do no harm to practice. Cleverly devised so that nobody's real name was used, the chosen society names all followed the sport of golf, a newly established popular sports pastime.

Mr Green, Mr Flag, Mr Argyle, Mr Dune, Mr Fairway, Mr Fore, Mr Tee, Mr Club, Mr Par, Mr Ball and Mr Caddy. If, no *when,* he successfully passed his apprenticeship, he would become Mr Caddy as the lowest ranking member. But still!

This was the exciting part - his inauguration! This would be the start of his own life, not one forced upon him by human hand or Fate. He simply couldn't wait to find out what was in store for him!

Reading aloud the handwritten words from the old scroll, multiple thrills shot through him. Solemnly promising that he would keep the Sacred Secrets silent; that Secret Society meetings could be arranged at his place of business; that he would treat all information he became party to confidential; and never *ever* discuss Society business with any member of the public, on pain of death.

Nods from the high-ranking men rippled around him: without even realising he'd been holding his breath, Nigel exhaled noisily. Celebrations broke out, carrying on into the late hours of the night.

**

Agreeing eagerly with his mission, Nigel didn't need to do much homework on his 'target'.

In recognition of his courageous action, Frederick (Fred) Field was well known in the area. His gallantry in saving the child from a certain death at the railway crossing won him sympathy for his ensuing injuries from all parts of the country.

His occupancy of the Crossing Keeper Cottage was wrong on so many levels! He shouldn't have been in such a job with housing as a reward after that accident had disabled him! Nigel's thoughts spat.

He wasn't alone in this thought, he knew; the Order of the Elite believed the same. The elderly, the disabled, the young... Nobody from any of those feeble categories deserved the rights of the able bodied!

Such people would be thrown into lunatic asylums if the Order had their way - all traces of them removed from society completely. They were second class citizens who needed to be reminded of their place, despite the calls over the last decade for free speech, free love and justice for all.

Anyone fighting against this belief became an enemy against their way of life - an enemy of the Order of the Elite was not a position anyone wanted to find themselves in. Some townspeople, upon hearing of their collective thinking, branded the group 'evil'.

Nigel snorted. When men of power and wealth ruled the world, everyone would learn to toe the line! That would also put women back in their place - the home. Women most definitely needed reminding that they were of a lower social standing than men!

On the subject of lines, the Railways had a lot to answer for! Ruining the beautiful countryside just for profits! Loud clanking and hissing engines that scared animals half to death shouldn't be allowed. As for the poor sheep or cattle on the line killed when a train came through - that was an inexcusable tragedy!!

How were animals supposed to know that the land they had wandered across for years freely was now a danger? Why should farmers have to fence off their land to keep their livestock safe? Did the railway companies compensate them for such an intrusion on their land? No. Of course not.

Blood boiling, Nigel's mind returned to his mission: his victim had to be taught a lesson. The railways and anyone associated with them were a curse!

Under cover of darkness, Nigel crept along the old trackbed on his way to the Crossing Keepers Cottage. As it was a route that he had taken many times, he could safely pass by moonlight without attracting attention from the light of a torch. Nobody from any of the houses on Sidings Way with a view of the old Station would see him if he kept to the treeline in the shadows.

With the Cottage looming, Nigel paused, playing back the plan in his mind. Touching the Apprentice badge on his chest as if it was some kind of talisman, he was all set. The weather was his comrade tonight, as the strong winds and heavy rain would muffle any loud noises. Satisfied every element was perfect, Nigel took a deep breath then advanced. Banging on the back door, crying out for help from within, he waited.

Reg hadn't yet gone to bed, noise from the wild weather outside had made him stay up later. Hearing the commotion at the door, he reached for Fred's old jacket before hurrying to answer it. Pulling the hood up and over his head, it fell almost beyond his eyes. Likewise the length of the garment draped almost down to his knees.

That didn't matter. If anything, it would offer him more protection against the inclement weather, Reg knew. Opening the door, in the blink of an eye and before he could see the person's outline against the horizontal driving rain, he was grabbed and dragged outside.

Thrown by this turn of events, Reg was automatically ready to fight, knowing now that the cry for help had been an ambush. Who it was and the reason why, he didn't know. Used to sudden fisticuffs breaking out amongst the boys in the orphanage, Reg had soon learned how to fight back, thus he could always give as good as he got.

Nigel was surprised by the man's ability to fight back, he had to admit, having believed that Fred's disabilities would mean he wouldn't be able to defend himself. Near the Cottage's garden well, both men were sent sprawling without warning when they slipped in the mud together. Pausing to get his breath after being winded by the landing, Nigel realised that he'd been lucky to avoid injury. He had narrowly missed hitting his head against the wall of the old well. The second thing he realised was that his adversary stopped moving.

Had *he* hit his head?! Was he unconscious... or dead?

Cautiously, Nigel leant over Fred's prone body: but there was no reaction, even as the ferocious storm raged around them. Kicking him brought no reaction either, so he knew that he needed to check for the man's pulse.

Tugging back the hood to get to his neck, Nigel gasped to see the man's motionless face staring up at him had striking mis-matched eyes. More importantly, shockingly so, it was not Fred Field.

Panic flooded through him. This wasn't meant to be a murder, it was only meant to be a beating!

Nigel privately knew, not that he could *ever* acknowledge the fact, that one of the members of the Order was a very high ranking policeman in this area. Ironically, he had a surname which fitted the given secret society names. At meetings, the senior members wore decorated face masks so that none of the potential new members could identify the men in the outside world, but Nigel had recognised the policeman's distinguished voice.

Not that this would be enough to save him from the law. This man would never give away his position to support Nigel: nobody in the Order would. Toying with the idea of not telling them, Nigel knew in the next instant that he had to as it was part of his mission.

That left him with only one choice. He had to hide the body until they could make a plan. But where - and how?! He hadn't the faintest idea how to go about it, and it wasn't as if he could ask someone for help either.

Calm down, he told himself, *think*.

His brain presented him with the answer after several long minutes - somewhere between the farm and the path, amongst the trees. Nobody would notice freshly dug earth *there*! It was genius; he congratulated himself for thinking so well under pressure.

The next question was, how was he going to transport the body to where he'd bury it? The quicker he got rid of it, the less chance there was of him getting caught. Nigel shivered with the realisation. *Focus*, he reminded himself.

Seeing the old wheelbarrow sticking out from some overgrown bushes at the side of the house, he felt victorious. It was the perfect transport: farm workers were often seen moving about this area with a wheelbarrow, even during the night. Nobody, if they did come across him, would question it.

Next he needed a shovel, and some sort of covering. Finding what he needed, Nigel headed for the place he deemed the best spot for burying the body, ensuring the cover wouldn't accidentally blow open. He doubted that anyone would see him on the short journey, but it wasn't a risk he wanted to take, he had to ensure the body was fully covered once it was in the wheelbarrow.

Shuddering at the magnitude of what had happened in the last ten minutes, and with the weather continuing to lash down upon him, Nigel tried to keep from panicking. Wind whipped up everything it came to, while rain pelted whatever was in its path.

Before heading home, he returned to the Cottage to check everything was exactly where it had always been. That included the old railwayman's jacket that usually hung by the front door. He'd remembered to strip it from the body before... he quivered as the memory rolled around his mind once more... dumping the body into the hastily dug grave.

No doubt Fred Field would have noticed the jacket was gone and immediately know something had happened, so it was a triumph remembering to replace it. Although soaked now, it would dry soon enough, and leave no trace of the outing.

Who was the mystery man? The question kept going round his head. Perhaps this man was Mr Field's guest. Nigel gulped. That gave him another problem - once he discovered the man's disappearance, Mr Field would report him missing. From there, an investigation would follow.

Keep calm, he told himself, *a plan will be worked out.*

If the members of the Order wouldn't, or couldn't help him, then he would work something out himself. But they were implicated also, every single one of them, having put him up to the task in the first place. Nigel felt better with this realisation. Pulling the Cottage door closed behind him, he smiled.

It would all be fine, he needed to have faith in the Order. Reaching to touch the society badge on his chest, he was horrified to find it missing. *No!!* His cry was lost in the wind.

Scouring the Cottage and grounds for any sign of it came up with nothing. Then, the thought struck him - it could have come off while transporting the body along the old trackbed. Doubling back to check, his efforts were to no avail. Despite the danger of being seen, he scrutinised every inch of the route until the torch batteries died.

Deep, deep trouble awaited him when he reported back without it. Nigel gulped once more.

An Observation

01:13 on June 25th, 1971.

Walking to the window as had become routine, the troubled insomniac watched the weather wreaking havoc over Ellenbrook.

Spying a figure on the overgrown path below, hunched over and wrapped up against the storm, the onlooker grows more curious upon seeing the figure is pushing a wheelbarrow. Hmm... Peering into the half-dark for a closer look, it is obvious the barrow is empty; no, wait, except for a spade.

Why does the mysterious figure carry no flashlight? Stupid not to at this small hour of the morning, let alone in such terrible weather! Brain skipping ahead, he concludes that the person is simply a farm worker, hurrying to finish whatever task he was doing and get out of the weather.

Sighing as he turns away from the window, the observer thinks nothing more of it, deciding to make a cocoa to nurse back in bed.

The Alban Way was bathed in moonlight. Sounds are smothered by the nightly hush, with the peacefulness broken only occasionally by the hoot of an owl.

As the dawn chorus awakens around the old Ghost Station hours later, only the wildlife detect there is something amiss...

Chapter 1

15:13 on February 5th, 2015.

The eerie whistle reached Mike again.

In the beginning when he'd been assaulted by the noise - it was THAT loud - all had been peaceful at the Halt. Could it simply be an ongoing joke being played on him?

Often, Mike waxed lyrical about 'The Golden Age of Steam'. Not that he was a trainspotter in any way... His subconscious told him that the sound belonged to steam trains of the past. As a man with an openly curious mind, Mike surmised this whistle would be the type to come from a Ghost Train.

In turn, this gave him an idea for a funny Halloween skit that perhaps, with work, could be a great video. Shaking his head with the thought, he put the idea to the back of his mind as he continued to work. Videos, photos, events... All of that was a *long* way into the future!

Nature had run riot over the common public cycleway path, now called The Alban Way, that had once been the track bed of the Hatfield to St. Albans Railway line. A local goods train service had run on the line for the last years of its use before closure in 1968. The last passenger train to travel the 6 mile track, taking in Hatfield, Lemsford Road, Nast Hyde Halt, Smallford, Hill End, Salvation Army Halt, St. Albans London Road and finally St. Albans Abbey, had been back in 1951.

This meant there were decades of near-jungle growth to tackle. Landowners over the intervening years hadn't been interested in any upkeep of the abandoned Nast Hyde Halt. Mike wasn't complaining, not really.

It was good, because this meant his 'mad plan' (not his choice of words) to renovate the Halt to its former glory was unopposed. Helping him in his quest was his solid background - a reliable and respected Royal Mail employee for almost twenty years, Mike was a local man with a good heart.

He took pleasure in talking with members of the public he encountered on his rounds: greeting them respectfully with 'Sir' or 'Madam', unless they knew each other then he used the friendlier terms 'Darling' or 'Buddy'. Everyone received a friendly smile from Mike and, mostly, he received one back.

Working at the Halt was no different - regular interruptions by well-wishers, walkers and cyclists were all things he had to deal with. It seemed everyone wanted to talk; most asked questions, curious about his plans.

He met people who both were and weren't from the local area, which puzzled him - some people had heard what was going on at the old Ghost Station and wanted to see it for themselves. As the saying goes, there's nowt as queer as folk... and didn't Mike know it!

Several people had asked what had given him the idea, most using the same words.

"Why is the local postman restoring an old railway station?"

Mike gave the same reply each time this was asked, so much so he was able to recite it without much effort.

"Cycling along The Alban Way to work every day, I was already aware of the area's history. The catalyst was when the St. Alban's railways began getting attention and I wanted the same for Nast Hyde Halt. However, without official support I knew it would be up to a private group to undertake the work. Unable to wait for this to happen, it became my project. It's time the town wasn't just known as the Hatfield University town."

Most people agreed with his statement, to Mike's surprise. Most praised him for undertaking the work himself, some remarked he was mad to do it alone. To all of them, he nodded and smiled.

One supportive trio, who Mike was used to seeing on afternoon walks along The Alban Way, stopped to admire his progress so far.

Privately, Mike thought that there wasn't much in the way of visible progress but he was heartened by the comments.

"How far do you intend to clear? From the Cottage to the Halt?" One woman asked him.

Mike shook his head. "Further up, to Deadmans Crossing." He corrected. "About half a mile in total."

"You know how it got that name?" One man asked him with a smile.

Mike's curiosity was aroused, sensing a story. He knew it was simply named after the farmer of the time, but he was happy to play along.

"Deadmans Crossing *is* an unusual name, it sounds like it might have sinister connotations. Does it?" Mike had one eyebrow raised in mixed interest and disbelief, as was his trait.

From the group's expressions, he was in for a good story, and there was nothing Mike liked more than a fascinating tale, even if he knew it was fictional! Taking the time to listen, he wasn't disappointed by the man's account, ensuring he gave an appropriate response.

**

Mike thought it fitting on the restoration to use the old tools of his grandfather's that he had inherited a few years previously.

The project was something his grandfather would have loved to have been involved in - and this way, he was. The broom's wooden handle had long since worn smooth in places, with several chips and scratches adding to its character.

Despite this, it was sturdier than any of its modern counterparts; the same went for the bequeathed saw and sheers in Mike's arsenal. Investing in a new set comprising a pruning saw, two variations of gardening secateurs and a lopper, he was ready to go!

At the rate of an hour each day after work, as well as any other spare time he had - not that he had much - he began to calculate how long the restoration might take. It would be many, *many* months, if not several years.

Truly, he wouldn't know how much work was required until he had unearthed the old platform and could then determine how much damage needed to be repaired. Whatever he found, hours of hard work would be undoubtedly required, but he was no quitter.

At least the platform had been upgraded from the wooden original to brick after 1923, otherwise there might not be anything left to restore! Something he'd read then came back to him. Up the line, the old Salvation Army Halt was created from wooden sleepers soaked in tar. Most of it had lasted the test of time, perhaps proving that builders and engineers of the previous century knew more than they let on. Nowadays, nothing made from wood could last that long, due mostly to vandalism and theft.

Mindless thugs, Mike shook his head with his thoughts. When adding decor to the Halt, he'd have to bolt things down to thwart any attempts to 'borrow' them. Thankfully, not everyone was Nast-y! Mike smiled at the joke.

Judging by the amount of people already admiring his work and his grand plan, there were lots who were grateful to him. The old Halt was becoming a part of the Ellenbrook community once more, and taking Mike with it.

Having started out with the idea to restore a natural local beauty spot, and then working with the railway's history, he certainly hadn't foreseen these additional benefits!

Chapter 2

Surveying the scene, Mike concluded there were *mountains* of weeds and debris!

Naively he'd thought because he already had cleared a great deal he had broken the back of the task - but standing back to survey the site as a whole, you could hardly discern the change!!

Setting his jaw defiantly, he knew this was nothing he couldn't conquer alone: it would take continued muscle and more man-hours, that was all. He had plenty of both and with no deadline for the project to be finished, his theory was that it took as long as it took.

His train of thought was interrupted (no pun intended) as he saw a smiling young couple heading his way. Bracing himself for an onslaught of questioning, Mike returned their smile.

"I thought we should say hello. We've been watching you for a while now." The man began.

His partner rolled her eyes. "Way to go Jay, real creepy." She hissed at him before turning to Mike. "We live in Sidings Way," she explained.

Mike nodded. "You can see everything from that street."

"See, I told you he'd be cool." The man retorted, hating the way that his partner had made him look bad. Seeing that she rolled her eyes again, he frowned.

"You're here to ask questions, right? Go ahead." Mike tried to get the conversation back on track. (Literally! He smiled at the thought.)

They both shook their heads, with the woman elaborating. "We're here to help."

"Thanks, but it's not necessary." Mike replied instantly.

"Oh," the couple exchanged looks.

"Well, we wondered if you would like to store your tools in our garden. It would save you carrying everything on your bike back and forth every day." The man spoke after a minute, inclining his head towards Mike's mode of transport, currently leaning against the cycleway hedges.

"We don't mind: we don't use our shed. It's just full of cobwebs," the woman added.

"We should introduce ourselves," the man said to her. "Mike isn't likely to trust two strangers." He stretched out to shake Mike's hand. "I'm Jay, and this is my wife, Lucy."

Mike nodded. "Pleased to meet you both."

"The path is very narrow in places, perhaps your bike would be safer at our place too?" Jay offered, looking around them.

Mike hesitated. As much as he didn't want to intrude on anyone's property or time, he acknowledged that it *would* be handy to have a safe place for his tools - and his bike.

"I'm sure it is safe around here," Lucy began, "we've never had any trouble in the area, but you can't take chances, can you?"

Inclining his head thoughtfully to one side, Mike gave the idea serious consideration. What the couple said made a lot of sense.

"When you're finished for the day, if you're not in a rush, you could come and look at the shed." Jay tried. "It has a working lock and a strong, solid door. Being at the end of our garden, nobody would see what was in there. In fact, hardly anyone would see you coming and going."

Mike's face broke into a wide smile as he decided to accept. "If you're sure you both wouldn't mind,"

"Of course not." Lucy cut him off. "We'll watch for you coming."

"It doesn't matter how late it is." Jay added.

"Sweet." Mike nodded. "That's a great idea, thank you both very much."

The couple laughed kindly at his gratitude.

"You haven't seen it yet." Lucy smiled at him.

"I'm sure it'll be perfect." Mike smiled back. "You're right - it'll save me swerving all over the place trying to balance stuff on the bike. I can be far more productive this way."

They all exchanged smiles again.

Consulting his watch, Mike informed them that he would be there in around an hour's time, thanking them again before they let him get back to work.

It wasn't accepting help, as such; it was purely a practical arrangement. As much as he knew he may need help with some of the heavier things to do with the restoration, most of the necessary work he planned to complete solo. This was *his* project, therefore meriting his hard work and nobody else's.

Having worked as part of a team in his first job after his schooling finished had taught him lots of things. His boss had taught him an awful lot about DIY, life lessons that every youngster should have included in their education. These skills he'd used at home with his parents, and then when he was a homeowner himself - now he was honing them at the Halt!

Mike had always wanted to do something that allowed him to help people; affecting their lives for the better... He wasn't afraid of the highs and lows of having responsibility placed on his young shoulders. Sensible and determined, when he had a plan, he stuck at it and worked hard to achieve it.

This was the case with his potential new job. Being a member of the Royal Mail was a high honour, and fitting into village life as their postman was what he set his heart on. Some areas of Hatfield fitted this bill, meaning also that he wouldn't have far to commute, so he investigated what applying for the job required.

An extremely nervous 22-year-old Mike sat the necessary entry exam a short time later, passing with flying colours. His triumph increased when he was allocated a dream village to work in. Provided he followed Royal Mail protocol, and adhered to the tight timescale, he was effectively his own boss.

Suddenly getting up early in the mornings to go to work was a pleasure not a chore. The 5 mile cycle to and from the Post Office Depot base kept him fit for his village rounds, and for life. His dog Harvey loved going on long walks, and thanks to his increased fitness, Mike enjoyed their time in the great outdoors more.

Chapter 3

Several weeks into freeing the Halt, Mike started to see a real difference. Passersby also commented such, giving him a surge of pride and boosting his strength.

It hadn't escaped him that similar restoration projects would have a team of workers and a pool of resources. Plus, those projects were completed much faster. Ah well, Mike shrugged with the thought. He was confident in his abilities to learn the necessary skills as he went along.

There were instructional videos online for just about every task known to man, and available for anyone to view as many times as required in order to get the job done. Specialist skills like those of electricians and plumbers he would never ever attempt, but everything else Mike treated as fair game.

One skill he foresaw learning was bricklaying, assuming the original platform bricks would need to be replaced. Thinking about bricks, Mike knew there would soon come a time when he would need to buy supplies. Bricks and cement, fencing for the platform and paint for the edging were vital. Small things such as plants, compost, grass seed and the like he could afford out of his own pocket.

More expensive supplies would require funding - he knew fundraising was the lifeblood of such restorations. It was something he would have to champion in order to reap the benefits at Nast Hyde. Decor too would be an expense, but a justifiable and enjoyable one.

Naturally, his mind had jumped to decor the moment he'd begun the project. Mike wasn't averse to hard work, but that was the bit he had a feeling he would *really* enjoy. Suitable decor, or railwayana as it is more recently known, had increased in popularity over the years - alas, this meant that prices were spiralling. Not that there would be much room at the Halt once the project was finished, but the usual railway paraphernalia was imperative!

Starting with signs - No Trespassers; Beware of Trains; Stop Look Listen; etc. He smiled with the thought of making one that warned about the Ghost Train. Perhaps there would be room for vintage travel posters or those fabulous retro metal advertising signs! Mike lost the rest of his time that day to his thoughts...

After almost five weeks, finally the platform was exposed once more. Mike paused to lean on his trusty broom for a moment.

"Nice one!" he said to himself.

Although the area's previous trackbed was now referred to as The Alban Way, a cycleway and footpath, it wasn't overly wide. Once tamed, Mike knew he would need to widen the cycleway and path further to gain the best from the area. That would be a lot of work, and he was relieved that he had chosen to only complete a half mile stretch at Nast Hyde!

In his imagination, he could see the project complete - he had done since Day One. But now everyone could see the fruits of his labours. Laughing as one youngster stopped to tell him that his work was done, Mike corrected him on this point - this was a journey that was far from over.

Colour wouldn't only come from the decor, Mike decided. As he had disturbed nature, it was fair to encourage it where possible. The word for it was rewilding or maybe just wilding, he wasn't quite sure, but either way he intended to lend nature a hand.

Lots of different birds swooped and sang around him, so his focus began with his feathered friends. The first vitally important thing to do for the area's wildlife was to ensure their habitat.

Birds were known to like blackthorn, hawthorn, dog rose and bramble as they all made excellent nesting. As these were plentiful, Mike made a mental note to destroy as little of these as possible in the continued clearing. Deciding then also to install some nesting boxes, he began to think about all the wildlife he'd possibly encounter.

Grass edging between the cycleway path and the platform was a good place to start, along with plants to brighten up the platform area. As yet, he didn't know what - it was something else that would require researching. He knew a little about gardening and plants, knowing that bulbs looked after themselves and Daffodils would provide a golden welcome year on year.

Apart from when the misty murkiness brought signs of the old Ghost Train back, that was... Laughing out loud with the thought, Mike knew he could have a lot of fun at the Halt.

Chapter 4

As Mike was too far from home to use his own water supply, initially for the grass but it would be required for all of the new plants *and* on a daily basis, he realised he needed a local source.

Relying on someone else for the water supply wasn't fair. It wasn't right to intrude on anyone's home many times to fill his watering can and he would absolutely hate to 'put anyone out'. People became aggressive or took liberties after time, alas Mike knew this from experience. He sighed wearily.

One saving grace was the arrangement with Jay and Lucy for the shed. He was able to come and go as he pleased without disturbing the couple, an agreement that suited all parties involved. It was such a simple idea of theirs, but a huge help!

In a flash, the answer came to him - the Ellenbrook stream. Burbling water reached his ears from the other side of the road to the platform by the old Crossing Keepers Cottage. What a joyful sound! No wonder some people used it as part of their relaxation routine: he could see the attraction, whale music not so much!

Following it, Mike learned that the stream ran through a short tunnel in front of the Cottage to the other side of the property before coming back into Ellenbrook Lane. Not far away was the local police station, and around 100 yards fell between the Cottage and the old Halt.

Hopefully the stream would grant enough water for the plants, and nothing too disgusting at the same time! Mike smiled with the thought.

The railing around the drop to the stream told of a potential danger to life, and it was indeed a problem. How could he get a bucket safely down the 5 foot drop into the reasonably fast flowing stream?

After a minute or two of musing, the answer came to him. A length of rope, or a really tough garden twine, or even string maybe, could be attached to the handle so that he could lower the bucket into the water. That was easy! He'd placed several items in the shed that he knew he didn't yet need, but might at some point - strong garden twine included.

Ensuring that every day he watered the newly sown grass seeds before leaving for home, Mike was thrilled to witness nature working magic when lush, green grass appeared in no time at all along the length of the path beneath the platform. It was a sight to behold!

Choosing a flat area of ground before the platform, Mike determined the best place for a sign and information post. He had already decided that a wooden post would be most appropriate, and be complementary to the surroundings - *and* the history of the old Halt.

The sheer weight of it, and the fact that it also needed to be theft proof, meant concreting in the post was mandatory. That would require a large hole, in depth anyway. Bringing his spade from the storage shed, Mike began to dig.

Finding a rhythm, of sorts, as he had to wipe the sweat from his brow several times in the July heat, he stopped when the spade hit something unyielding. Investigating carefully because he neither wanted to damage the spade nor break anything that might be of historical value, Mike gasped when he brushed what he'd encountered free from dirt.

To his horror, he saw it was the bones of a human foot.

Soon swarms of police took over the site, arriving from both the local police station 250 yards away *and* the bigger station at Enfield.

Watching from behind the police cordon, Mike wondered exactly what they would unearth. How many more bones would be found? More than likely it would only be a few. It was common to find various animal skeletons buried when an area backed onto farm land, and this had no doubt been the case over many decades. It had been his first thought when he saw the bones, until he realised they were of a human foot.

Despite himself, he shivered. There *was* a possibility that it could be the body of a whole skeleton, indicating a terrible accident had occurred. Or maybe... Maybe it hadn't been an accident - could there have been a crime committed in the vicinity?! Mike shivered again. Surely not. Any crime would have been reported in at least the local news over the years, and he would have seen, if not heard, about it. Regardless, *if* there had been a scandalous crime committed here, people would still be talking about it years later.

Whatever the story, it was the job of the police to find the truth. He would play his part in helping them to achieve justice, of course. Initially he had thought he may discover unusual things long forgotten, but he had never *ever* thought that might include a body!

Chapter 5

Mike's usually unruffled demeanour was disturbed as the skeleton was released from its earthly grave.

He watched the team of police as their many hands made light work of clearing the area surrounding the gruesome discovery. Whilst horrified by what had been discovered, at the same time he was also intrigued.

Why bury a body *here*? How was it done - and when?

More to the point, who would do such a terrible thing?!

The Officer who had first arrived at the scene noted Mike had been watching: he stood in a relaxed pose, with an expression that was horrified yet curious. Clearing his throat to bring Mike's attention back to the present when he hadn't moved as the Officer stood by his side, he began to speak when Mike's eyes found his.

"Mr Izzard, you will need to come with me to the station to write a statement about the discovery." The pregnant pause meant the Officer was waiting for an answer, Mike realised then.

"Of course, no problem. Let me just put stuff away and I'll come to the station." Mike hesitated as the Officer's rigid expression did not change. "It is okay to put my tools away first, isn't it?" He swallowed hard.

Escorted to an awaiting police car, and taken to the Enfield station in silence, Mike felt like *he* was a criminal. He'd never before been in a police car, or in a police station for that matter.

Then the thought struck him - why Enfield? Hatfield's local police station was literally across the road from the Halt. What did this mean?

On his rounds, he always nodded and smiled at any passing police - policemen and policewomen - they always similarly greeted him as they went on their way. But that was it.

This was completely different.

TERMINATION AT THE HALT, GHOST TRAIN MURDER MYSTERY

Arriving at Enfield Police Station, the Officer opened the door for him, walking side by side with him to the front desk. First, he signed some paperwork before instructing Mike to do the same: without hesitation, Mike signed his name several times.

It is mere formality, Mike told himself, trying to calm his rapid heartbeat and racing thoughts. Nobody was blaming him for the skeleton; there were procedures to follow after such discoveries, that was all. Right?

He swallowed hard, nodding as the Officer informed him that they would go to an interview room next. Escorted to a small room, Mike was surprised to find another policeman already there.

Sitting down as he was bade, Mike was introduced to Detective Chief Inspector McFarlane, before being encouraged to state what had happened. As his tale unravelled, with interruptions as he was questioned in between, he could see the men thought his plan was more than a little crazy.

Breathing a sigh of relief some time later, Mike knew he was off the hook. He saw that the Officer and DCI McFarlane both thought that it was obvious Mike wasn't connected in any way whatsoever to the skeleton.

Phew!

A lover of murder mysteries and crime drama, Mike had seen many police interviews that had turned unpleasant, or even torturous, when the police didn't hear what they wanted to. But of course that was all for TV, scripted specifically for extra dramatic effect, none of that actually happened. In real life, the police followed the letter of the law as well as enforcing it as was their job.

DCI McFarlane nodded with his thoughts. Most restoration projects unearthed findings that required investigation, and not only in the countryside either. It tended to be - if there could be a pattern - the older the site, the more mystery it contained.

"The Forensics team will remain in the area for however long they consider necessary. As long as you don't disturb them or intrude where they are working, I will allow you to continue your tasks at the site." He smiled at Mike.

Grinning in relief, Mike nodded, knowing his time would be spent with half an eye on proceedings up the platform. Well, it wasn't every day you got the opportunity to watch a team of Forensics experts doing their thing!

"Thank you. Once I saw it was a skeleton, not only a few bones, I feared I'd be banished from the site for a good while. Of course, if that was what had to happen, then I wouldn't have objected."

The Officer and DCI McFarlane nodded.

"I promise I won't interfere with their work, and if they need me to do anything, they have only to ask. Nothing is too much trouble," Mike continued.

This was met with more nodding.

"Do let us know if you unearth anything that might be of value to the investigation." DCI McFarlane left him with.

"Of course, yes." Mike nodded keenly.

Encouraged to sit back and relax, he didn't have to wait long until his typed statement was ready. Placed in front of him to sign, he was reminded to first check the text for accuracy so that he agreed what it contained.

After this, Mike was then excused. The Officer took him back to Nast Hyde in the police car before disappearing once more.

Mike let out his breath slowly. What a tale to tell!!

His mind was filled with so many questions, but they were all unanswerable, he frowned with the realisation.

It wasn't exactly police protocol to update a witness, thanks largely to falling numbers of manpower, but he had an inkling it wasn't the last time that he and DCI McFarlane would meet.

Would he personally get involved in the investigation of the Nast Hyde skeleton? It was more likely if he managed to find any clues that the police had failed to find. Perhaps there would be other things buried at the site that would turn up. Hmm...

Chapter 6

The local gossip mill *really* cranked up seeing Forensics set up their white canvas tent over the area surrounding the skeleton.

Everyone and anyone local 'just so happened to be taking a walk' through the area at least once, stopping to talk with Mike. This happened so frequently, he was becoming used to the interruptions.

"Found a body?" Most asked him, keeping their eyes on the ominous white tent.

"Skeleton." Mike confirmed, his attention split between the person and the police after being asked the same question repeatedly. "From long ago, by the looks of it."

At this, jaws dropped open and eyes bulged: the speaker's attention nearly always returned to Mike then. "You *saw* it?"

Mike nodded, adding further horror by making his confession. "Yeah - I got the fright of my life when I dug out a foot!"

The other person in the conversation at this point either shuddered or nodded; some went deathly pale and then excused themselves from the conversation that instant.

Many went on to speculate about the skeleton's story, in nonsensical ways. Was the mystery skeleton a beaten housewife, or an escaped prisoner? Perhaps a farm worker caught red handed doing something wrong, or a jilted lover out for revenge? The list was endless.

Mike, amused by the workings of the human mind, played along with their theories, always ending the conversation with the same words of wisdom: "We'll find out in time."

Once finished some time later, Forensics packed up and disappeared without even so much as a nod in his direction. Mike shrugged to himself. The local press no doubt would have a field day with the finding...

**

TERMINATION AT THE HALT, GHOST TRAIN MURDER MYSTERY

Following protocol, police sergeants worked the area, going from door to door to check facts. However, as it was an investigation into the death of an unknown person from an unspecified time period, nothing of any use was gleaned.

Several procedures were ruled out because of the lack of details around the skeleton - but there was one line of enquiry they could pursue: the *very* long, tedious list of Missing Persons. The usual procedure to ask friends and family about the reported person missing was one avenue that the police in all likelihood couldn't go down; no doubt there wouldn't be any remaining family to help piece this puzzle together.

There may be cousins or siblings with the same DNA as the skeleton, but the amount of time that the body had been buried meant any remaining traces would be miniscule. Such family members may not be easily found if they had moved from the area, and changed names.

It would take an awful lot of time to investigate, and represented a lot of legwork for potentially very little or no gain. DCI McFarlane called a temporary stop to the investigation, knowing the Coroner would take over the next part of proceedings. Crossing his fingers for the results to come in from there, all he could do was wait ...and hope. Should the death be ruled as a murder, then a painstaking, slow search was required.

**

Through his tidying and tying back, digging and clearing, cutting and cleaning, Mike found all sorts of hidden things - but none as worrying or as newsworthy as the skeleton.

Old coins, some pre-decimalisation; a multitude of different sized misshapen pieces of metal; lots of general rubbish and the odd Roman piece of pottery deeper down, but nothing of real interest. Mike was surprised to find himself disappointed by the 'haul'.

Perhaps Nast Hyde had no more secrets to surrender: no sooner than he'd had the thought, he saw something. It was a man's cufflink, inscribed with an 'X'.

The old adage of 'X marks the spot' made him laugh when he thought that if it had been several metres westwards it could have been some sort of marker for the skeleton. That would have been spine tinglingly spooky!

It *could* be a personalised cufflink, but the 'X' may simply signify a lover's kiss. On closer inspection, Mike could see the letter had been etched into the cufflink's smooth central raised surface carefully. This was no mass-produced item - someone had taken real care.

He couldn't tell what metal it was made from, but it would have been an inconvenience to the owner who had lost it. He had decided when he first started the project to keep anything of potential value and interest he found buried, in the hope of reuniting such things with their owners, no matter how long it had been since the loss.

Most of the things he had uncovered while digging and clearing were made up of weeds, roots, leaves and plants; abandoned nests; spiderwebs; creepy-crawlies - both alive and dead; buckled beer bottle tops and rusty bent nails. Lots of them. Between those and the multitude of misshapen metal, he wondered if those finds were railway related.

Pausing every so often, he was always listening - mostly for the whistle of the Ghost Train, which he'd heard regularly since identifying it. Automatically he listened also for the distant click-clack of a train on the track, but the euphoric 'whoosh' of a train rushing by was lost forever.

Sometimes, he mimicked it with the broom in an over melodramatic fashion. Those who knew him and of the restoration project said that Mike should have been a railway child!

He had to admit, the police investigation had helped greatly in releasing the Halt from nature's strangle-hold. The group of policemen had cleared that specific area faster than he could have done in a fortnight! It was almost a shame that they hadn't discovered a reason to clear the whole area...

Mike shook his head to banish the thought, that was not something he should be wishing for! What if he'd been forced to stop work? Or worse, banned from doing any more of the restoration?!

Shuddering, he wished he could take back the thought. Whatever had happened to that poor person buried here was a tragedy. Mike had learned first-hand that there wasn't much justice in the world nowadays, but that didn't stop him wishing for it.

Chapter 7

Mr Don, the Police Area Coroner, took over investigations when a body was discovered. A basic check of the skeleton showed that the hole in the fractured skull was the probable cause of death. This meant it had been either accidental or murder.

None of the other bones were cracked or broken, to signify serious injuries. This was a skeleton in very good condition, considering. It was a virtual impossibility to find a whole skeleton, but this one was as complete as he had ever seen.

After more examination, he was able to conclude that it was the most complete human skeleton ever found in the country! This did not help to identify the victim needless to say, but all was not lost. Even without any hard evidence to work with, and an estimated time of death from years ago, there was still hope: in the form of a specialist they always turned to in such situations for help - a Forensic Odontologist.

Any dental professional who furthered their training in this way could display Dip. F. Od or D.F.O. after their name, and the police database of said specialists was a useful resource in cases such as this one.

Mr Don himself had worked with several of these named go-to professionals in the past, therefore, he was able to choose the most experienced man for the task in hand. Not only would he help using his specialist knowledge, but he could also concur with Mr Don about the cause of death and details of the skeleton. It wasn't the done thing, but Mr Don had a feeling it would happen regardless.

Truth be told, Mr Don hadn't dealt with a lot of skeletons in his career. Identifying the difference between male and female skeletons was the first thing to do. Commonly the pelvis was used as a reference, although there were other ways to differentiate between the sexes. If the skeleton had a shorter and wider pelvis, that indicated it to be female. Having made the measurements already, this one was male.

Generally, there were three categories to determine the age of a human skeleton. He knew that human bones still grew until the person reached thirty years old. This one, out of respect he referred to it as a 'John Doe' - the common name for an unknown person - was in the 'young' category.

With the specialist due to arrive early the next morning, Mr Don and his assistant were at work before their regular start time of 8 am in preparation for the visitor.

"Mr Don," said Jo, the young woman who was his assistant, and also his daughter, interrupted his thoughts. While working, he insisted that they referred to each other professionally.

He could see there was another shadow in the hallway with her, and smiled to see that Dr Zohan had arrived promptly.

"Thank you Jo, you can show the Doctor in."

Extending his hand as the older gentleman entered the room, he saw recognition in the man's eyes.

"Mr Don, a pleasure to see you again!" Dr Zohan beamed.

"The pleasure is mine." Mr Don smiled. "This is an interesting case that I believe is right up your street." Gesturing to the table, he saw Dr Zohan's face light up. "An almost perfect one; decades old. I know you'll be able to give us answers."

"Excellent!"

Dr Zohan shrugged off his coat, and marched to the sink to wash his hands. This done, he reached into the bag he'd placed on the floor as they had shaken hands, emerging several minutes later with the items he'd sought.

"So what can you tell me?" He teased, a familiar twinkling in his eyes and a smile twitching his lips.

"I would say the skull injury was undoubtedly fatal. But that alone doesn't determine whether or not this was murder. Most of the burial site was untouched for decades." Mr Don paused. "I suspect our John Doe's death is suspicious. An accident would have been reported, and the body would not have been buried."

"Perhaps." Dr Zohan mused, studying the skeleton for a moment before he looked up. "This skeleton is a 'young', between twenty and thirty years old. I'd say more towards the twenties. No fractures to other bones, so it is a possibility that he was not involved in a fight for his life prior to death."

He paused while scrutinising the skeleton more.

"Perimortem trauma from time of death shows no sign of healing, therefore is the cause of death."

Mr Don watched as Dr Zohan bent to study the teeth of the skeleton closely. The room fell silent apart from the noise of the two men breathing, which seemed, in the circumstances, strangely wrong. Shaking himself from the thought, he concentrated on his counterpart.

"If this skeleton *is* over four decades old, then it will be almost impossible to identify."

Mr Don looked at him fearfully. "The dental records database surely will come up trumps?" It was more of a question than a statement.

Dr Zohan shook his head. "I'm afraid not. Obtaining information from the dental records database will be of no use in this case. Assuming - not that it is ever safe to assume anything - your John Doe was recorded as a Missing Person."

Mr Don looked at his counterpart quizzically. "That is the only way we can find out this young man's identity." He almost wanted to stamp his foot in annoyance at the rebuff.

"Records are kept up to a maximum of thirty years." Dr Zohan explained, lowering his voice.

"Dammit!" Mr Don spat.

Chapter 8

Mike kept thinking about the poor person who had died at the Halt. Of course, maybe this wasn't the actual place of death... The thought was somehow comforting.

Maybe the range of overgrowth provided perfect cover for the body, after all it is said that the best hiding place is in plain sight. Had this been the thought of the murderer when he, or she, tried to dispose of the body? Whoever it was, they had chosen well as it had remained buried for a lengthy amount of time. That made him wonder how long it took for a human body to decompose?

He supposed as the area had been untouched for decades that the skeleton could have been buried since the closure of the line in the late 1960s. Was the death associated with the railway, or was the burial site chosen coincidentally?

Forensic police tests would pinpoint an accurate timescale. His knowledge of police televised dramas told him. Mike knew motives for murder tended to surround two themes: love and money - jealousy and attachment. There were times when the tormented turned on their tormentor. Sometimes it took *years* before one snaps and sees no choice but to murder their torturer. Most murderers who hid their victim's body often felt a compulsion to regularly check on it, which usually led them to making a mistake - in turn giving vital clues to pursuing detectives.

Was he morbid to think that the skeleton had been a murder victim? For some reason, his mind kept returning to this outcome, although there was no proof - yet. Did his liking of TV police dramas influence his thoughts? He had been told often throughout his life that his imagination was vivid.

Once the timescale had been established, perhaps a witness might come forward. It was a low probability, he knew, as the more time passed the less people on the whole tended to remember.

Police protocol for finding a dead body started with friends, family, colleagues in order to build up a picture of the victim, including their usual haunts. Technology was used to trace car, phone, credit and bank card records. But for the skeleton, they couldn't do *any* of that.

Mike thought back over the history of the Halt. It wouldn't have taken long after the line's closure for nature to establish a sprawling grip over the area.

Moving the body would have taken two people, or one with a mode of transport, but getting a vehicle down the trackbed would have aroused suspicions. No, that can't have been right. So, that left horseback, or a trolley, or some kind of trailer. Whatever mode of transportation was used, it was still a *very* risky thing to do. Of course, it would have been done at night, no way would it have been possible otherwise.

Around that time, there would have been staff labouring on the nearby farms at both Nast Hyde North and South. Not many passersby paid attention to labourers going about their business during the day - but at night, *that* was different. Surely someone would have seen something? It couldn't be as impossible as it all sounded.

Mike shook his head. He wasn't the right person to solve the mystery. And yet, because the skeleton had been buried at Nast Hyde Halt, he felt a compelling sense of responsibility for finding out the story behind it.

As one of the local postmen for many years, Mike knew the people in the area well. He recognised when surnames didn't match addresses, and more often than not was able to redirect any wrongly written address details on mail so that they got to the right homes.

On his usual rounds the following day, the thought came to him that when his skeleton - he now referred to it that way - was named, he might already know the family!

Wouldn't that be something?! The thought of being able to bring peace to a family mourning the mysterious disappearance of a loved one from years ago gave him renewed hope of the investigation succeeding.

Work took up his thoughts and energy for most of the day, until his regular late afternoon cycle home. He still referred to it as 'going home', although his stop off at the Halt was another mile from his home.

How many families did he know of in the area who might have a relative of the era of the skeleton? If his grandfather had still been alive today, he would have been able to tell Mike all about that time. Rubbing his fingers over the grooves in the handle of his grandfather's old saw in his grasp, his thoughts remained on the older members of his family as he worked.

**

Over the last six weeks that he'd spent sorting out the area, he had finally dug out the whole platform. Relieved to see it remained in a reasonable condition, Mike now knew it would take only replacement brickwork and a lick of paint to smarten up.

Only! He laughed to himself, if there were hundreds of bricks needing to be repaired or replaced he would be presented with another huge job! There and then, he hoped that it wouldn't be a high number.

Trying to look on the bright side, as he tended to do, he had the thought that at least if there were masses of bricks to be replaced, he would develop expert bricklaying skills! Whatever number it was - high or low - it'd all be worth it in the end.

The hard work that sometimes seemed never ending would all be worth it. On the days where it all seemed too much, he kept telling himself it would all be worth it. So much so, the saying became his mantra.

After a new station sign and relevant decor were installed, the Halt would be returned to its former glory. The large platform station name sign would have been wooden back in the day, and therefore *should*

('should' being the operative word, he thought to himself) be easy to replicate in his workspace at home.

He sighed. It was a damn shame there wasn't any track left... not that this affected the Ghost Train. The thought made him smile.

His beloved dog, Harvey, ran to him as Mike entered the kitchen at home later that night. Stooping to make a fuss over him as usual, Mike's mood lightened. No wonder dogs were man's best friend - they were always pleased to see their humans.

Mike had the idea then that if he was Station Master, then Harvey was Station Mascot. It was the very least his best friend deserved!

Chapter 9

His knowledge of nature was varied and extensive, but Mike knew it wasn't enough to ensure the perfect habitat at Nast Hyde alone.

He had known that in the olden days - and occasionally now - some plants were used for medicinal purposes; some were poisonous; some functioned only to attract pollinators to ensure their species survived. Ensuring he had the right blend of such native plant life for Nast Hyde would be down to trial and error - and research.

Most common garden flowers were known to attract bees and butterflies: they were a good place to start. Ideas were in abundance throughout the different gardens of the streets he regularly walked. Hmm... It gave him a lot to think about.

Reading about poisonous plants was enough to put him off trying wild food, although most people ate bramble fruits as they grew abundantly in the wild. Yet he knew that flowers have been added to the human diet for thousands of years as chefs experimented with edible flowers.

Mike wasn't surprised to see the most common edible flowers were regularly seen in gardens - Dahlia (water chestnut/spicy apple/carrot), Hibiscus (sweet citrus), Honeysuckle (sweet nectar), Pansy (fresh tasting), Jasmine and Rose (sweet and floral, Geranium (citrus/nutmeg) and Sunflower (mild nutty).

Thinking about food was making his stomach growl, so he stopped his research to grab a bite to eat before continuing. Had farm workers in the olden days eaten wild foods when they were out in the fields all day?

It was known that the Cornish pasty had been created so that the working miners had something to sustain them during their shifts. The thick crust meant that they could hold the foodstuff without needing to wash their hands first, which of course would have been impossible. Although nowadays a pasty contained one set of ingredients, in the sweet or savoury category, they had been historically made in two parts - one side savoury and the other sweet, to act as a main meal and dessert.

As a lover of the area of Cornwall, Mike had eaten more than his fair share of pasties, especially his favourite, the traditional ones. Like many people, he didn't envy the jobs those brave miners did years ago. Thankfully his work at Nast Hyde was nowhere near as dangerous as working down a mineshaft!

**

Making his final choices very carefully, he set about positioning the plants to spread throughout the half mile stretch he had commandeered from nature.

Most of the horsetails and ferns, various fungi, non-flowering plants, mosses and lichens already in the area weren't disturbed by Mike's work, as well as a variety of wild flowering plants. He was most relieved to not have to start from scratch for the whole half mile site!

Having made records since starting the project, Mike could compare the most common butterflies and moths in this area against those in the country as a whole. He was astonished to learn that our winged friends of the plant world were important to show the health of the surrounding environment, giving benefits including pollination and pest control.

The Painted Lady, Peacock, Marbled White, Meadow Brown, Gatekeeper, Common Blue, Small White, Large White and Small Tortoiseshell butterflies were more prevalent, with only the Gatekeeper in low numbers at Nast Hyde. Moths were different: of the eight listed, only three were regulars - the Emperor, Elephant Hawk Moth and the Cinnabar Moth. Naturally, butterflies are always easier to distinguish because they are typically larger and more colourful than moths.

Of course, while working around the area, he kept an eye open for any clues that might appear. Every time he had to dig a hole, he half expected to make another discovery. Perhaps it would be linked to the skeleton, perhaps it wouldn't...

Always making sure to rescue any straying caterpillars on the cycleway and path, Mike gently relocated them to a safer place - bushes, plants or amongst the grass. Most could easily escape in emergency situations, but out of all of nature's bugs, insects and creepy crawlies, caterpillars seemed to need the most human intervention.

Nothing creeped him out, not even the most commonly feared of the group - spiders. Mike could pick them up with or without his gloves on, watching with fascination as they went on their way after his 'interference'.

Whatever the creature in peril, Mike would do his best to remedy the situation for all concerned. Did this make him the David Attenborough of Hatfield?!

Chapter 10

Mike's eyebrows raised higher the longer DCI McFarlane spoke. They had determined that the skeleton was of a young man, then in his twenties. Due to the nature of the injuries sustained, they were treating his demise as suspicious, although the crime had been committed over forty years ago!

"Not much evidence survives that long, I don't suppose," Mike spoke thoughtfully.

"Indeed!" McFarlane agreed. "However, if you think you find something relevant, bring it over and ask for me."

Mike chuckled, tickled by the idea of going on a clue hunt. "Like an old knife or some bullet casings, you mean?"

"There weren't any bullet holes." McFarlane shook his head. "Trauma to the back of the head was the likely cause of death."

"That doesn't sound accidental." Mike shook his head. "Poor man."

"We never had any doubt that it was an accident. That's why we're treating it as suspicious. It is likely that most of the young man's family will have passed on or moved away. Nonetheless, a nationwide statement will be issued instructing anyone who thinks they may know the identity to come forward."

Mike nodded. "Once the name is known, the family will be found. There must be someone wondering about the disappearance of their loved one."

"There might not be," McFarlane hated to burst Mike's bubble, but he agreed with Dr Zohan that it was almost impossible to identify the skeleton. He also agreed with Mr Don's thought that this was a skeleton of a long ago reported Missing Person, so there was a glimmer of hope. "Not every person who goes missing has someone in their life to miss them. Some just have an employer who easily replaces the person who never turned up again. Some aren't even officially reported missing." His voice took on a defeated note.

It caused Mike to wonder how many such cases were never solved. Memory of the cufflink came back then.

"I only found one thing of interest, a man's cufflink, with an X on it. It wasn't in the same area, though it might be around the same age: it was fairly tarnished."

"Hmm," McFarlane mused. "It could be connected, but I'm not sure. Don't lose sight of it. Did you clean it?"

"Yeah, a bit." Mike hesitated, knowing then that he'd probably done the wrong thing but he had to be honest.

McFarlane clicked his tongue in annoyance. "Forensics won't get anything from it now you've cleaned it."

"Sorry." Mike apologised, feeling chastised by the DCI's tone. "I didn't think it would have anything to do with the body, the skeleton, I mean. It wasn't in the same area. Plus, they didn't use cufflinks in those days as commonly as they do now, or from the nineties?"

"You're probably right." McFarlane nodded, withholding his sigh. "If you find *anything* else," he emphasised, "don't even wipe the mud off it before you bring it in."

"Okay. Will do." Mike answered quickly. "Sorry." He added again.

Exchanging goodbyes not long afterwards, Mike muttered "lead" audibly. That was the shortened version of the phrase: 'That went down like a lead balloon!'

**

DCI McFarlane jumped on Mike's idea of finding local residents still living in the same area from around forty years ago.

Tracing back two generations, it was easy to research the meagre few names he found. Alas, it was in vain. With no elderly relatives to help, they now needed to tackle the puzzle from another angle. So, perhaps someone in the same age group - a colleague, a friend, a member of the same club...?

Approaching it a different way, how would they garner any suspects now the death had been ruled suspicious? Usually, murder investigations have potentially several or lots of suspects - but this case had none!

Would it simply be too difficult to solve? McFarlane snorted with the thought, hating the idea of adding to the already stupendously high unsolved case pile. He was proud of his unblemished record - chalking up no unsolved official cases throughout his long police career.

Avoidance of adding to that pile was a thought at the back of his mind whenever there was another murder reported anywhere in the country. The world contained enough in the way of mysteries.

Now, the unfathomable story surrounding the Nast Hyde skeleton threatened his record.

Chapter 11

Feeling like he was starting to win the ongoing battle to uncover the platform's surrounding area, Mike smiled.

Harvey might have been good at digging random holes in the garden and in the fields, but he wasn't much practical help at the Halt. Nonetheless, he kept his master company - delighting in the extra attention from visitors that came along reasonably frequently.

It pleased him to see that his human was a popular figure in the community - lots of smiles and gestures of hope and gratitude told the story. Harvey knew human emotions, and the differences between them all.

There were lots of unusual smells in the area, even more so where Mike unearthed soil that had been undisturbed for years. Every time Mike stopped to examine something more closely, Harvey stuck his nose *right* into Mike's gloved palm to explore the finding. It was never anything he could eat, so he soon lost interest, but the fact never seemed to dissuade his human from continuing to dig...

"We had a dog like yours when I was a child." The man's voice interrupted Mike's reverie as he paused (or was that paw-sed?), in his work.

Mike nodded. "They are an intelligent breed."

"Took a liking to my Dad's pigeons." The man smiled at Mike, as if on cue a pigeon swooped over their heads.

"Wow. He must have been a real pigeon fancier! Did he race them?" Mike asked, his attention fully on the man.

Harvey had stood up from where he lay to get maximum attention from the man who'd stopped to talk, being rewarded by having a fuss made. When it stopped, he'd hopefully looked up at the stranger, but saw his attention was on Mike now. *Ah well*, with a quiet sigh, Harvey lay down again.

"He had a loft - thirty racing pigeons, all of them champion stock. Some of them were prize winning." The man's gaze went beyond the landscape in front of them. "Get a bad rep, pigeons." He nodded as another swooped over their heads to land in a nearby tree, with the first bird.

Mike nodded again. "I like them. People say they are disease ridden pests, but that's wrong. They are one of the cleanest birds, *and* there is little actual evidence that they're significant transmitters of disease. But people don't care about the truth, they prefer the myths."

All of a sudden, the man came out of his memories and back to the present. "That's so true!"

Grinning at him, he extended his hand, introducing himself as Alec Stimpson. Shaking his hand, Mike introduced himself in return although he thought that everyone knew him - at least, the people around the Nast Hyde Halt area did.

"The local pigeons now recognise me." There was a note of pride in Mike's voice.

"Of course they do!" Alec replied. "Did you know they're among the cleverest of all birds, being only one of six species able to recognise themselves in a mirror? They can also remember people who are unkind to them. That's why they recognise you, they know that you are a good one." He smiled at him.

"Feeding them helps!" Mike joked, and they both laughed. "It's such a shame pigeon racing was fazed out, I'd have liked to have seen it myself. It must have been quite a sight to see them flying home, sometimes from as far as 1300 miles away. Not to mention their amazing work in messenger services during the World Wars."

Alec was contemplating what he was going to say next, Mike could see. Would it be another trivia titbit? Their conversations were more like trading knowledge than chatting.

"I learned recently that they can reach altitudes of 6000 feet, and the fastest recorded speed by a pigeon is 92.5 miles an hour!"

Mike inhaled sharply. "That's faster than I've ever driven." He admitted, laughing.

Alec too laughed before his expression turned thoughtful. "There were many pigeon clubs in London, back in the day. I can't imagine how much fun they would have had! It is said that Charles Darwin was one of the top club's most famous patrons."

Mike nodded. "That doesn't surprise me. Darwin's book 'Variation of Animals and Plants Under Domestication' has two chapters on pigeons, but dogs and cats share a chapter. Most people would think it'd be the other way around."

Alec gaped at him. "I didn't know that!" He studied Mike's expression for a few moments. "I know Tesla also enjoyed pigeons. He was inconsolable after his favourite, a white female, died."

Mike smiled. "Here's me thinking I was daft to properly bury a poor pigeon I found here a few weeks ago."

Alec smiled kindly at him. "That's not daft, it shows you have a big heart." He paused. "Speaking of burying, any news on the skeleton?"

Mike exhaled slowly, shaking his head. "There's no news yet. I'm not sure they'll ever find out what happened. If it was a long time ago, there wouldn't be much in the way of evidence left."

"A terrible business, whenever it happened." Alec shook his head.

They both watched as more birds swooped into the area, aware Harvey was also keeping an eye on the comings and goings of the area's wildlife.

"Well," Alec broke the silence that had fallen between them after a few minutes, "I suppose I'd best leave you to it." He stooped to pat Harvey again, telling him. "You and your master are doing a great job. Keep up the good work!"

Chapter 12

It was a long shot, a *very* long shot, DCI McFarlane admitted to himself, but it was possible he knew the identity of the mystery skeleton already.

Leaning back in his chair, he allowed himself the luxury of time to reminisce. His mind returned to the time he was a local bobby walking the beat, and a young man whom he'd personally known for many years suddenly disappeared. Over time, he had wondered if they would ever discover what had happened to his friend.

The man's name was Reg Reynolds, and he was a relief Signalman/Crossing Keeper in the Outer London area. Reg had grown up in a London orphanage - another poor child alone in the world, without even a distant third cousin to link him to a family. His love of railways had blossomed from an early age. Reg told his story one day when McFarlane stopped off at the Crossing Keepers Cottage for his now regular cup of tea and chat.

Not ideally situated behind the locomotive shed of their local railway terminus, the orphanage building trembled as gigantic steam engines roared by. Most children were frightened by the hissing of steam, the clanging and clunking of metal and tools; voices shouting above the din; the cloying smell of oil and grease; clouds of soot and steam; and on occasion, sparks rising into the air. But not Reg.

It fascinated him. None of the obvious dangers instilled any fear into him; if so, his curiosity outweighed any concerns he might have initially had. Many railway workers shared similar stories, as most starting their railway careers - as long as they were young and fit - began with shunting. This was the moving of trains and carriages between yards and platforms, Reg had explained, seeing that McFarlane was confused by the railway term.

Alas, this was a perilous workplace. Anyone who got accidentally trapped between rolling stock could be crushed to death. It happened more times than it should have. Injuries most common of all were to the many workers who lost digits or limbs in shunting accidents. Reg shook himself at this point, as if to waken himself from a dream of a past memory. Continuing with his story, Reg explained that he wasn't considered strong enough to be an engine driver or a fireman, so his place of future work was never going to be as exciting as on the footplate of a steam engine.

Learning the ropes of working a signal box in the area, Reg found that their lofty perches gave him a high and clear vantage point to watch the line and the trains, as well as not being too physically or mentally taxing.

Proving his worth came easy, but Reg hadn't wanted to remain in one solitary signal box for his whole life, so he joined the relief team, learning also all about operating railway crossings as he encountered jobs on the ground as well as above.

DCI McFarlane came back from his reverie. Despite Fred, the railway station's Crossing Keeper, being made redundant in 1968 when the last goods train rolled by, he was allowed to remain a tenant in the Cottage. Fred had kept in touch with several fellow railwaymen, including young Reg who had in later years taken over duties in his absences. As per their previous arrangements, when the Cottage was empty Fred always asked Reg to stay to keep an eye on things.

It had been in the late summer of 1971 when newly promoted Sergeant McFarlane had taken a distress call from the Crossing Keepers Cottage. Fred had returned from a week's holiday to find no sign of his friend and former colleague. The usual fire in the grate which heated the whole Cottage had long since burned out, signifying that it had been quite a time that Reg had been away.

There were no indications of a break-in, but even stranger still, all of Reg's belongings remained - including his old camera that he never went anywhere without. His unexplained disappearance was so out of character that Fred was *convinced* something untoward had happened.

McFarlane shared his fear, instigating a search of the Cottage and the surrounding area. Hours later they reluctantly gave up, no further forward than when they'd begun. Reassuring Fred that he would report Reg as a Missing Person, McFarlane could remember writing the report as clearly as if it had been yesterday. What happened next, however, was unprecedented.

Not only lecturing that there was no evidence to support the claim that the man was actually missing, DCI Woods ripped up the report before sending McFarlane out of his office with a flea in his ear.

Following a night's lack of sleep frustrated by his superior's attitude, as it was obvious that foul play had happened, McFarlane decided he would complain to the Area Chief. Knowing that the senior policeman was due to arrive for a regular monthly station meeting the next day, he had to choose his opportunity carefully. The result of their meeting was one that remained with him, along with the betrayal of his superior's destruction of the Missing Persons report.

Having listened to McFarlane begin the story of their missing friend, Chief Irons cut him off.

"I don't know why you are wasting my time with this, Sergeant."

"It should have been reported yesterday, after we returned from the search." McFarlane began. "I wrote out the correct paperwork, but DCI Woods tore it up."

"Do you dare to suggest that your superior officer has committed an offence?" Anger came over the older policeman's face. "He acted appropriately *and* followed police protocol. There was no evidence to suggest something had happened, despite what you might think."

"B-but..." McFarlane stammered.

"You will apologise to DCI Woods!" Chief Irons stormed.

McFarlane knew he had no option. "Yes, Chief Irons."

"Don't ever insult any of your superior officers, again! Do you understand, Sergeant?"

McFarlane hung his head. "Yes, Chief Irons."

"I'll hear no more on this subject. If I catch you talking about it again, you will be dismissed. Instantly dismissed. Do you understand?"

McFarlane's heart sank, he visibly sagged. "Yes, Chief Irons." He replied meekly.

"Now get out of my sight!" The Chief bellowed.

McFarlane scuttled out of the office to resume his post on the front desk, where a colleague had been standing in for him. He kept his head down when his superiors passed on their way out of the police station an hour or so later.

Once his shift was over, McFarlane stopped at the Crossing Keepers Cottage on his way home to update Fred. They vowed to do their best to find out what had happened to their friend, with or without police help. Were the senior policemen in cahoots? There was no obvious reason why, but both he and Fred knew their theory of something sinister going on contained more truth than they had originally thought.

In their free time, both men made enquiries about their friend. Sometimes together they talked to acquaintances to try to establish patterns of his behaviour; sometimes McFarlane worked alone. He started by looking up old case files of a similar nature when he knew his superior wasn't in the station to catch him. He kept his research to times when he was alone, not wanting to tempt fate that one of his colleagues might question him and report him.

Over the months that turned to years, neither of them were any further forward in learning what had happened to poor Reg. Was the answer now imminent?

Chapter 13

As well as documenting changes throughout the project with photos, Mike had set up his camera to record videos at different stages.

Not just taking note of what he saw, Mike was thrilled to hear an owl hooting in the background of several videos. It would be fantastic if the owl was to take up residence at the Halt - that would certainly add to the spooky atmosphere of the area.

Beginning to list the different wildlife he encountered at the Halt over time, Mike was amazed by the variety. Research showed that the Hatfield area had always been frequented by different wildlife species - many varied moths and butterflies, as well as seven different species of bat alongside the regular animals.

Frequent animals that had been sighted included water, bank and field voles; moles; harvest mice and rats; muntjac deer; foxes; grey squirrels; rabbits; common frogs and toads; hedgehogs; the extra special great crested newt; slow worms and grass snakes. Various creepy crawlies as well as dragonflies, damselflies, crickets, beetles and grasshoppers had made a home here.

Every colour in the animal kingdom was represented, or so it seemed. Silvery slithery snail trails sparkled in the dimming light, catching Mike's attention from even the most awkward of places - up tall trees and the wooden sign post, vertically across the platform brickwork... Did they use magic suction power to defy gravity?!

Other strange goings-on were captured on video over time, including the Ghost Train. Mike had been hearing the otherworldly steam train whistle regularly since he'd started work on the project, instinctively knowing what it was.

Remembering the information snippet he'd read after the first such event - he'd researched the sound to be absolutely 110% sure of what it was - he had discovered the first whistle on a steam train had been called a steam trumpet, as it was created by a musical instrument maker.

TERMINATION AT THE HALT, GHOST TRAIN MURDER MYSTERY

Over the years, train whistles had been continually modified until The Golden Age of Steam when the unmistakable warning crescendo had been perfected. Even people who didn't regularly travel by train knew the sound.

As if conjured up by his thoughts, the Ghost Train whistle rang out. Mike had been walking Harvey along the cycleway path that evening, allowing his thoughts to roam while his faithful furry friend sniffed around, exploring what had become his patch.

Suddenly, Harvey stopped in mid stride to hunker down. His alertness, with ears pricked and eyes wide, told Mike he also heard the approaching Ghost Train.

"Easy boy," he spoke gently to Harvey, squatting down beside him so as to reassure him: his permanently weakened right knee creaking in protest.

Harvey was quite familiar with his human's creaking and cracking, but kept his attention on that odd whistle. Where did it come from? Where was it going?

Scanning the darkening territory around them as the sudden storm rolled in, Harvey couldn't detect anything usual, despite all of his senses being on high alert.

For a time, Mike had wondered if the sound was in his mind. Barry, a videographer and fellow colleague, had asked him if there were any ghosts at the old Ghost Station, laughing when Mike truthfully replied 'yes!' Several other Royal Mail workers had overheard their conversation and from then onwards, they jokingly referred to Mike as 'Spooky Station Master'.

Brushing off their banter, and laughing with them at the ridiculousness of the whole ghosts, ghouls, vampires, pixies, fairies, elves, genies, witches and other supernatural concepts, Mike knew that there were lots of people around the world who *did* believe.

Certainly he believed in the Ghost Train - he'd heard the whistle while standing in more than one place; more proof that it *wasn't* his imagination. Plus, there were other mysterious things that kept occurring.

Not that he'd spoken about any of these with anyone else. Most people already thought he was mad to undertake the restoration, he didn't want them labelling him insane as well!!

Conversations at the Halt and at work turned to the supernatural after the skeleton had been discovered. Some people even went as far to warn Mike that the Halt was haunted and because of this, he should take extra caution. As a bit of a joke towards this attitude, he had a fluorescent safety jacket personalised with 'Mike, Station Master, Nast Hyde Halt' on the back. Keeping the jacket in the shed with his tools, a hard hat helmet, gloves and safety goggles reminded him to wear it while at the Halt. During summertime, it would act as a magnet for bees, wasps and flies. Wasn't it just as well he didn't mind any of God's creatures?!

Harvey pulled on the leash to bring back Mike's attention as the thunder clapped loudly overhead and heavy rain began to lash down. Home, *now!* - his actions said. Harvey could really move if he had to: this was one of those times. It was for the best Mike knew, although personally he loved watching the darkened sky of an approaching thunderstorm in the hope of seeing amazing lightning usually accompanied by thunder claps. Nature was truly magnificent, in all its forms.

"C'mon then boy, let's go." He agreed, allowing Harvey to lead them both home.

Chapter 14

As the storm continued to rage into the early hours of the next morning, Mike got up to comfort Harvey. Despite disagreeing with encouraging animals into a human's bed, Mike allowed Harvey in with him when the thunderstorm raged for most of the night.

Shocked to see his old friend struggling to jump up, Mike got up properly to lift him into bed. With the realisation, he saw for the first time that Harvey was ageing. It hit him like a tonne of bricks... His faithful canine companion was a valued family member. Harvey was his best friend in the whole world - being without him wasn't worth thinking about!

Between the upset surging through him of the notion that Harvey might not see the restoration finished, and the storm wreaking havoc outside, Mike had a very restless night.

The next morning was, of course, a weekday, so he wasn't able to inspect the damage at the old station until late afternoon. Of course, he could have got up a bit earlier and stopped off en-route...but he decided against that, for several reasons.

Throughout the day whenever he'd come across various scenes of destruction and storm damage on his rounds, Mike dreaded what he would find at Nast Hyde. To his horror, he saw that the wild howling winds during the night had been powerful enough to bring down trees!

Pouring rain throughout the storm left mass flooding all across the town, fortunately not flooding any houses he delivered to but damaging gardens, sheds and greenhouses. Holding his breath as he approached the site of the old station he'd spent the last few months painstakingly clearing and sorting, Mike gasped. Tangles of branches were strewn across the area, with some uprooted trees damaging the platform. The whole area was strewn with storm debris!

Mike groaned. It'd take at least another fortnight to clear the storm's destruction. Feeling defeated, the concept of abandoning his plan hit. It was the first time he had allowed the thought to enter his mind, despite all the naysayers telling him that the project was impossible. He believed in signs - was this one?

A sign to leave it be? Or a sign he needed help?

Worse - was it a sign of things to come? The thought horrified him. Would every storm desecrate the area?!

Bringing an assortment of saws and cutting tools for his future sessions at Nast Hyde, Mike worked on reducing the fallen trees and branches to a more manageable size in order to remove them safely.

This was the first time he encountered any heavy lifting at the Halt, but no doubt it wouldn't be the last. Thanks to keeping himself fit and strong, Mike was sure this was a job he could do alone, although he always ensured he had a backup plan in place before tackling any project.

Recalculating, he decided that it might be more like twenty sessions to return the site to how it was pre-storm. Thankfully there was no finishing deadline, Mike thought to himself as he walked towards the Crossing Keepers Cottage with his trusty bucket and rope.

Some of the grass had been torn up and some plants damaged, he saw to his dismay. Repairing what he could and making a note of what needed replacing, the idea of fundraising for latter restoration stages came to him.

Smiling as he reached the water source and lowered his bucket into the higher than normal stream, he requested that the Nature Gods reward his efforts. Mike liked nothing more than snatching victory from the jaws of defeat!

**

Over the numerous years of his career, McFarlane had worked on many Missing Persons cases, the majority of which had turned into cold cases.

TERMINATION AT THE HALT, GHOST TRAIN MURDER MYSTERY

It was perpetually frustrating! Throughout Britain, there were almost three thousand cold cases amongst the police forces: a disgusting number in anyone's estimation!

The key to solving Missing Persons reports had been the dental records database, back then and it was still effective in modern times. The printouts since the time that McFarlane began to use it had taken up reams of paper. Although it made up the bulk of one filing cabinet, as it was added to every month, it had proved useful on several occasions when the computerised system was down. Technology was great when it worked!

Indeed, it was something that had travelled with McFarlane up the ladder as his career had progressed. He'd had many colleagues and superiors inform him, over time, that keeping these files was unnecessary, but he had never parted with the records. He knew they could still be of use, despite their age and sheer size. Plus, always at the back of his mind was the mystery of what had happened to Reg...

As dental records were kept from a specific time period of between eleven to thirty years ago, their relevance declined in time as new records became available. Technological advancements for the police computerised Missing Persons reports system meant it grew more secure, and with user friendliness, faster - but McFarlane knew the large file like the back of his hand and, as a result, was able to produce what they were looking for with relative ease.

So... It was a distinct possibility those bulky files contained the dental records of the Nast Hyde skeleton! Starting the required communication with the Coroner and the case's Forensic Odonotolgist, he had all the necessary information to hopefully help pinpoint the skeleton's correct identification by the end of the week.

However, this was one job he would not be delegating. He owed it to Reg. He'd felt guilty from the start that something had happened, and he didn't know what it was! In a manner of speaking, he wanted to put his ghost to rest. Not that this was an announcement he could make: McFarlane knew he'd be called 'old and doddery', and worse, should the observation reach his superior, it would be a reason to bring forward McFarlane's retirement.

Besides, this was a task that might not take up too much time. He knew the whereabouts of Reg's file without a lengthy search; as it was a file he had thumbed through many times. Assuming the identification of their skeleton matched young Reg's file, that was.

Chapter 15

With the ongoing rain that week, Mike's thoughts turned to another disused station further up the old branch line at Smallford. A terrible place for flooding after heavy rain generally, he couldn't help but wonder what that part of the Alban Way looked like.

The local news had announced that this weekend runners were set to complete an annual charity long distance race, their route taking in the area. Checking details from where the race route was posted online, Mike was able to add a warning that the area was notorious for flooding and may be impassable.

Knowing that he could potentially help a lot of people if there was a real problem at Smallford, he prepared to lose a lot of the time he would have spent at the Halt that day. It was always best to both be prepared and plan ahead!

Setting off to see how badly that stretch of cycleway had been submerged, the crazy idea to take his flippers, beach shoes and wetsuit with the kayak struck. Loading the car for the few miles journey, soon Mike was presented with the worst flooding he'd ever seen!

Perhaps it wasn't such an insane idea to bring all that gear. In places, the water was too high to even see the path, never mind access it safely. Measuring, for curiosity as much as anything else, Mike was amazed to find that the deepest section of the 300 yard stretch of rainwater was 2 foot!

Mindful of the runners, and entertained by the notion of kayaking through Smallford station, he quickly donned his wetsuit before carrying the kayak and the rest of his gear down to the flooded area. Floating perfectly, even with a person's weight in it, Mike then had the thought of using his kayak as a 'ferry' for anyone who wanted or needed to pass but couldn't. Walking in flippers was difficult - well, that wasn't their purpose - but his beach shoes would protect his feet while towing someone through the depths! Plan made, his smile widened.

Even in these unusual surroundings, being in the kayak again reminded him of the many hours he'd spent beachcombing off the Cornish coast. Many of his childhood family holidays had been spent in that part of the world: most of his happiest memories were from there. Cornwall held a special magic for him, delivering the perfect combination of sunshine with reviving seaside sights, sounds and smells.

That was something that the coming of the railways made possible for more people - travelling to the cities, to the country, to the seaside. He wasn't the only person that loved spending their holidays at a British seaside resort. Most people dreamed of winning the lottery and going to live abroad, but Mike would happily have chosen somewhere along The Lizard Peninsula!

It wasn't long before the first runner appeared, startling him from his daydreaming. When their eyes met, both men smiled.

"There are two options," Mike began, pausing as he saw another few runners coming up behind the first man. "You can take a very long detour, but I'd imagine you have run enough by now."

The small group laughed at his words, but they all agreed!

"Or?" One man said.

"It's deep enough for a kayak?!" A lady dog walker appeared and joined the group peering at the large mass of water with mixed emotions.

"In places, yes." Mike told her. "You can get in one at a time and I'll take you across." He offered, to the group.

"I don't think so." The lady shivered and turned, retracing her steps.

"You're sure that it is safe?" One younger man asked.

"I wouldn't advise going through it yourself." Mike made reference to their attire. "Not without waterproofs. Your shoes and socks would be ruined, plus that would lead to cramps and blisters and all sorts of problems."

Murmuring throughout the group rose. There was still a confused air amongst them.

"I'll go first, then you can decide to follow or not." After five minutes of contemplation, the first runner made his choice.

Several runners from the back of the group had also turned around and retraced their steps, taking what Mike had indicated as the long way around. He shrugged to see them go. He was here to help, because he knew he could, but he wouldn't force anyone to get in.

"Okay." Mike smiled at him. "Easy does it." He said as the man put one foot in first then the other, keeping his balance successfully until he sat down.

Testing the seriousness of the situation, Mike spoke to the group before taking up the slack on the rope.

"No singing 'Row row row your boat', okay?" He grinned.

Much hilarity ensued. The first of his passengers laughed so heartily the kayak shook. Keeping his smile, Mike towed his precious cargo across the stretch of water at a steady but sedate pace. Steading the kayak while the man got out at the other side, Mike was thanked as the man headed off safely. The other runners cheered.

Ferrying them all took most of the next half hour, then there was a lull. Knowing the race times, Mike guessed he might be required for a while yet, so he bided his time. Whilst waiting, several more dog walkers had appeared and everyone was happy to chat. Some of them knew who Mike was, and conversation turned to his plans for the Halt.

Astonished by this - Smallford station was about a mile up the Alban Way from Nast Hyde Halt, but even so! - Mike realised that his project was affecting more than just the locals. Humbled by the amount of praise being heaped upon him, he was rescued by the appearance of more unsuspecting runners. Relaying again the two options to the next group that had been stopped in their tracks, most of them also chose to have a free ride across the water.

Two friends from the runners stated that the day was already unforgettable, but this was the icing on the cake! One dog walker and her dog took Mike up on the offer once the runners had all safely navigated the obstacle, telling him that it brought back memories of how on her and her husband's Italian honeymoon the gondolier had sung to them. Mike smiled, and replied how magical that must have been. The lady agreed, but made him laugh when she said that she was glad the smell of the Venetian canals wasn't present today!

Chapter 16

Later that day, Mike reminded himself that although there was a lot of work to be done thanks to the recent stormy weather, at least the Ellenbrook area wasn't flooded.

Sunlight highlighted something lodged in the bank of the stream beneath the usual spot where Mike fetched water, attracting his attention. As it wasn't something he'd seen before, he surmised it must have been exposed by the storm. Intrigued, he worked on trying to free it. Did his attraction to the shiny object indicate that he had been a Magpie in a former life? He almost laughed with the thought.

It came to him then that perhaps a clue or two, or more, might have risen to the surface post-storm. That reminded him to keep an extra look out for anything unusual. Perhaps this, whatever it was, would be a clue!

A visit to 'his' shed - which fortunately hadn't suffered much damage in the recent storm - yielded sufficient tools to cobble together for a makeshift grabber to free the item.

Tangled in what looked like muddied plant matter and other indescribable stuff, Mike finally managed to extract what looked like two pieces of some kind of metal. Dunking the pieces into the bucket's water, he retrieved each one at a time now they were cleaner to see what they were.

Both were very old, he could tell once he'd cleaned them properly. They both looked like badges of some sort, with a picture etched into their surface. He doubted they'd been out in the elements for long. Had they been dumped recently, or been buried in a garden long ago but washed away by the recent storm? Or perhaps they had been long forgotten and only now risen to the surface after being lost a long time ago. Nature moved in mysterious ways...

Thoughtfully, Mike pocketed them and walked back with his newly replenished full water bucket, intent on investigating the finds further when he had time. On his way back to the platform, he was stopped by an older couple who were grinning at him.

"You're the kind man with the kayak!" The man began.

"I thought you looked familiar!" The lady smiled at him.

Mike's smile turned to a grin. "I was happy to help." He shrugged off their praise.

"Nobody else would have done that." The man shook his head in wonder. "It could have been very dangerous."

"It looked like you were prepared." The lady frowned.

"Coincidence, that's all." Mike informed them. "Always happy to help out someone in need, if I can."

"There were thirty people as 'someone in need' this time!" They corrected him together.

"There should be more people like you in the world." The lady added.

Mike could feel colour coming to his cheeks. "That I agree with," he replied, "but I was taught to do my best by everyone. To be fair, I wasn't sure how much help I could be until I arrived at Smallford."

"You were amazing." They both spoke again together.

"I took photos," the man continued, "I'll get a set printed for you."

Mike was grinning again. "Sweet! That'd be great. Can I pay you for them?"

The man shook his head. "There's no need: I want to. I did laugh at the name of your craft."

The lady frowned and turned to her companion. "I didn't see it, what was it called?"

"The Old Buoy." The man replied. "Ingenious!"

Mike just smiled.

**

Sitting down to research the badges he'd found the next rainy night, Mike discovered that of the two, the smaller one was actually an old button. His plan was to be sure of what they were before he told DCI McFarlane of the finds.

He felt a strange pleasure to see that it seemed to be a uniform button. It was a real piece of history! Internet research would slim down the options of what it could be, and how old it actually was.

Most peculiarly, his other find wasn't the same. Created from enamel, the design on this badge had more detail. Although he couldn't clearly read the wording, he could see details of a crest in the centre of the piece. It was definitely a badge of some kind, perhaps from a group or business. The crest now made sense.

Returning to the button and researching further, Mike was jubilant to discover it was from a railway uniform. A bona fide link to the Halt's past, how exciting!! Could it have been from Frederick Field's uniform when he was Crossing Keeper at Nast Hyde Halt?

The thought came to Mike that perhaps the pieces had washed upstream from the old Well situated in the grounds of the Crossing Keepers Cottage. Despite it being long since boarded up, a surge of post-storm rushing water could have loosened anything that had been stuck somewhere in the vicinity for a while.

Much to his frustration, Mike found a gaping hole in the available information, even after thorough searching. How was this possible in this day and age of *everything* being on the Internet?!

When the Great Northern Railway (GNR) became the London North Eastern Railway (LNER) in 1923, uniform badges and buttons were simple brass 'LNER' lettered designs from the 1924 to 1936 period. The British Railways (BR) 'Wheel' design was used from 1949 until 1963, and came in two sizes depending on where it was on the uniform - 16.5mm and 25.5mm. The Pre-Corporate 'British Railways Logo' came into play from the Beeching era, 1960s.

Beeching! That man had a lot to answer for, closing down hundreds of stations, calling for the abandonment of 5000 miles of railway track across the country. Mike shook his head. How different would life be now if this hadn't happened? How many more railways and lines would be in action every day? How many towns that had been cut off with the closure of their railway station would be in a better position today?

The nearest historic preservation railway to Nast Hyde was the Epping Ongar Railway, although there are one hundred and thirty such volunteer-run steam railway preservation sites across the country. Offering hands-on experiences, alongside the traditional travel on their steam and diesel trains and vintage buses - truly this was a railway lover's paradise. A visit to such an organisation was high on Mike's wish list. The full immersive experience sometimes offered the chance to drive one of the old steam trains, now that would really be something!

This was along the same idea he had for the Halt, although bringing the past into the present was severely limited here. It reminded him that across the country, a number of railway stations proudly featured an old railway coach (or several) cleverly converted into restaurants. Some were even decked out like the old British Belmond Pullman railway dining cars, with every attention to detail perfected through restored fixtures and fittings from the 1920s. Amazingly, there are still Excursion trains to whisk their passengers back to the glamour of vintage travel!

Privately, Mike thought the best idea was to refashion old coaches into accommodations. He smiled to see examples of this were rented out for enthusiasts' holidays, or used as second homes! It blew his mind to imagine having an address beginning with The Old Railway Car.

Mike had been amazed to discover (during a search that had gone off on a tangent, as these tend to do!) that Network Rail occasionally sold off property when no longer required. Such sales came with certain restrictions and rules, but if everything worked out, it was possible that you could live in an old railway station. Now that was a thought!

Coming from his thoughts, Mike looked again at the button. Peering closer, he determined it depicted the BR Wheel, meaning it was from the latter period. That made sense, as it would therefore tie in with the uniform of the 1960s. How thrilling to confirm his initial thought!

Chapter 17

Invited to organise his first Nast Hyde Halt fundraising event together with the other former stations along the Hatfield to St. Albans branch line, Mike jumped at the chance.

The specific date was chosen to celebrate the 150th anniversary of the line's opening back in October 1865. Including a brass band, a fun fair, bicycle stand, pet shop stand and burger van in the local area, he created a display tent showcasing old photos both from the line and the area. Difficulty in parking at Ellenbrook was a major concern, so Mike set up road signs, directional arrows and 'slow down' signs on warning cones along the roadside.

All in all, the event raised £700 for upcoming necessary restoration repairs! Not only had the Open Day been a success for him, Nast Hyde Halt had been reported as the busiest station along the old branch line!

When the Mayor surprised everyone with her unheralded arrival, Mike arranged for lots of photos to be taken. Despite hearing nothing from her office about her availability for the event, he had half wondered if she would arrive. Publicity was key to raise funds and awareness, and he knew it might be something he could call on in the future. Large events might require multiple seating at tables, but he had contacts who could help - including the Royal Mail Delivery Office where he worked. Now he was getting approval from the Mayor, that would open up many doors.

Most gratifyingly, scores of people wanted to talk to him, whether they were new to the idea of his restoration or had followed his progress from the start.

Of Mike's many visitors that day, the men that stood out the most were local history authority, Roger Taylor; and Roy and his Dad, Fred Field's son. *The* Fred Field! Never in his wildest dreams had Mike imagined meeting a descendant from the heyday of Nast Hyde Halt.

Roy gave Mike a lot of information to help with the restoration. Learning about this extraordinary man - Fred's family, his health, etc - Mike always thought of Fred and his family whenever he looked at the old Crossing Keepers Cottage from then onwards.

Speaking of remarkable men, Mike was humbled by Roger's interest in the project, stunned when he asked to be kept in touch with all the updates! Years ago, Roger had co-authored a book entitled "The Hatfield and St. Albans Branch of the Great Northern Railway". The local railway was obviously a cause close to his heart: he and Mike shared a passionate and informative conversation before Mike had to see to the needs of other guests.

Fervently, he hoped Roger would remain in touch, getting an idea there and then that it would be great to bestow upon him the honour of opening the finished Nast Hyde Halt restoration!

**

Thinking about large pieces to 'dress' the top of the platform, Mike began to wonder about some sort of series of planters. There had been a wooden waiting shed taking up a lot of space on the old platform during the line's heyday. This had been demolished in 1951 to be replaced by a railway workers hut, which was removed eventually.

He was astonished when the chance of a lifetime presented itself not long afterwards. When a deal fell through between the local council and a local business sponsorship for brightening the town's manically busy Comet Roundabout, Mike was told he could take the huge plant containers to 'recycle' at the Halt - on one condition. Holding his breath while the condition was stipulated, Mike agreed straightaway, although he hadn't the faintest idea how he was going to manage it...

However, the offer was too good to turn down, so, setting his mind to the task he devised a plan. A 5 o'clock in the morning trip, with his Dad in his car and Mike driving his own car, would fetch the two rather cumbersome cubed containers, tying one onto the roof of each car, so that they could satisfy the condition to arrive and leave without disrupting the traffic!

Next, Mike turned his attention to the main station sign. Traditionally, the wooden sign had been hand painted, with letters carved in relief in order to stand out. Each railway group of lines had a set colour to identify the line, to help people differentiate - Nast Hyde Halt was regulation Oxford Blue to signify it was part of the Eastern Region. Thankfully, it was not a colour that was difficult to obtain.

As autumn was overtaken by winter blowing in, Mike wasn't put off continuing with the restoration work. In fact, with his postman background meaning he was out in all weathers, it gave him the best experience for colder working conditions. This meant to a large extent, his work rate wasn't affected by howling winds or falling temperatures.

Having slid on a patch of lethally slippery leaves during his commute one morning, Mike paid extra attention to clearing the pathways of as many fallen leaves as possible. His bruises and grazes from the fall reminded him, long after they'd faded, of the dangers of wet leaves. To think that the general public used to castigate the railways when 'leaves on the line' was said to be the excuse for postponed or cancelled trains...! Now, Mike knew that it wasn't an excuse, it was a feasible reason to be cautious.

As a backup plan, he had a few items kept to one side to do in his workspace at home. Mike wasn't daft enough to try to continue when everything was frozen solid! Thus he could maximise his time spent on the restoration. Even better, he and Harvey could enjoy home comforts when the location was the shed!

Chapter 18

Eerie screeching from bats flying around the area add to the spooky atmosphere at Nast Hyde, especially as the days shortened and darkened with the changing of the seasons.

Universal acknowledgement of these mammals centred around 'ghostly', but unconcerned by this, Mike wanted to learn about the seven different species of bats noted in the area. Even their names were alluring - noctule, natterers, daubentons, serotine, brown long eared, soprano pipistrelle and common pipistrelle. He knew a few humans who could be referred to as 'natterers'!

Beginning to wonder about having the Halt legitimately declared as a haunted Ghost Station, notably as he experienced unusual goings on, aside from the Ghost Train. Like when he had the feeling someone was behind him, but nobody was there. All the times he'd heard his name being called could be attributed to someone calling to their dog, or child, with a similar name - Tyke, Ike, Spike... he failed to come up with any other rhyming names. Or when things were tampered with overnight - but that could be attributed to mischievous youngsters.

Most things had reasonable explanations behind them, yet... The other-worldly whistle proved there was more to this than meets the eye. Look at how Harvey had reacted in the storm when the whistle rang out! It was commonly known that dogs hear at a higher pitch than humans, so the theory stood that they'd hear the Ghost Train whistle before any human could - they might be able to sense things before humans were able to. Media stories appeared all the time about dogs detecting dangerous health conditions in their humans before they actually knew themselves.

Then there was the skeleton! How could he forget?! Was the victim murdered here and now haunted the place, looking for revenge?

His brain jumped ahead. Those poor souls who were buried in mass graves from the County Mental Hospital at Hill End, a few miles up the track from here, did they haunt the place? Inexplicable things happened in the grounds and in the buildings there, surely? When the Nast Hyde area's large houses became military hospitals after the Second World War for wounded service personnel - they also must experience happenings that couldn't readily be explained?

Mike looked up with the thought, just about able to see the top of the House from the Halt. Rumour had it that Nast Hyde House was a model for Dickens' 'Bleak House', and to his pleasure, Mike had discovered a railway story about the famous author. He tried to recall it, sure that at some point he would converse about it with someone.

On June 9th 1865, the locomotive hauling the train Dickens was travelling on derailed after crossing over the Staplehurst viaduct. Fortunately, the coach he was travelling in - the first and only one - remained upright. He had recorded in his diary that he rescued fellow travel companions who were "much soiled but otherwise unhurt", before returning to the coach for his manuscript, 'Our Mutual Friend'. - What a man! Mike shook his head with the incredulity of the thought.

However, after consulting the list of accidents in the public Railway Archive, Mike learned the incident recorded in Dickens' diary was misleading - as there were 49 recorded injuries and 10 fatalities. So much for 'otherwise unhurt'!

Out of curiosity, Mike scanned the list for any record of incidents along the Hatfield to St Albans line, or any of the local lines. He discovered two.

On January 7th 1957, the Welwyn Garden City rail crash was caused when one passenger train ran into another after signal ignorance in fog! The second was closer to home in Hatfield, where a freight train went through the buffers on a spur line and into an overline bridge abutment at about 30mph, killing two people and injuring one.

That one needed translation: Mike was mostly au fait with the glossary of railway speak, but some things he didn't understand. A spur line related to a very short branch line. The overline bridge abutment he correctly guessed related to a supporting structure for a bridge. The precise terminology within the answer was just as confusing - substructure at the ends of a bridge span supporting superstructure for a bridge carrying roads, driveways, farm access tracks, footpaths and the like. It was no surprise that most fatalities due to railway accidents involved the staff in the engine cab, usually the driver and/or fireman, however at times the guard was as vulnerable as his colleagues.

Steam railways were still in their infancy at that time. Stephenson's 'Rocket' became the first official steam engine after beating four competitors in the October 1829 Rainhill Trials. After this, the first British branch line was the Liverpool and Manchester Railway of 1830.

It was funny to think railways were considered *the* technology of the 19th century. Without this undoubtedly brilliant invention, what would have happened to the transport of the world? The question wasn't unfeasible, as the railways took over from stagecoaches and horses in not only this country.

Most railways were built for necessity - both for freight traffic (which was referred to as goods traffic until the 1940s) and for passengers. It came as no surprise once passengers were introduced to the smooth, faster transport of the train they much preferred it to arduous, rough, bumpy journeys usually endured by stagecoach.

Businesses too preferred the railway to transport their parcels and mail, it proved much safer and quicker than by stagecoach. Following this, the Royal Mail added to their business by creating the travelling Post Office - something else linking Mike to the railways!

Even Royalty chose the train for their long journeys. There was a special Royal train made for the family, but it was also put into service for any special visiting dignitaries to the country. Was it really worth the expense of a Royal Train? Mike found out, again thanks to the wonders of Internet research, exactly how this had come about.

(To think that when he'd needed to do research in his school days, he had to go to the library and read microfiche on their specialist equipment, if it wasn't contained within the great tomes on the shelves!)

Queen Victoria was the first British monarch to travel by train to Windsor Castle from London Paddington in 1842. The locomotive had, as well as its usual staff, Mr Isambard Kingdom Brunel to assist. The Queen saw travelling the country as her duty, whereas monarchs didn't necessarily think that before - according to one historian.

The GWR (Great Western Railway) built a new royal saloon in 1874, replacing it later with a new Royal Train of six coaches for the Diamond Jubilee of Queen Victoria in 1897. GWR did not have the monopoly on Royal travel, and other companies followed suit by building Royal saloons for the special visitors over their lines.

The London, Midland and Scottish Railway (LMS) company built three armour-plated saloons for King George VI as he travelled to parts of England that were under bombing raids during the Second World War.

Mike was astounded to read that during that era, the existence of the Royal Train was still a state secret! It must have caused the secret services headaches at times: every Head of State has several attempts made on their life during their reign throughout history.

Royal Train carriages - and locomotives - were painted in a rich burgundy colour known as Royal Claret, the livery of the Royal household. Considerably updated for Queen Elizabeth II's Silver Jubilee celebrations in 1977, when not in use the locomotives work other services, but the carriages forming the Royal Train are stored in Wolverton Works.

Mike paused in his research. That name rang a bell. Finding the information he partly recalled, the names were similar. Queen Victoria had purchased Sandringham for the then Prince Edward when he married. The local station of Wolferton became a Royal Station, but it sadly fell victim to another of Beeching's axes, as the last service ran in

1969. Now the Queen has to take the Norfolk train to Kings Lynn and complete the 7 mile journey by road!

Sixteen of the GWR crack expresses (an express train between two named stops) had miniature chocolate machines installed in the 1930s. He wondered if the Royal Train did also. Usually tea urns and rock cakes were the only sustenance on offer for travellers.

Ah, a nice cuppa! That was what he could do with right now!

Chapter 19

Mike often thought about the beautiful steam engines of 'the good old days'.

At the time, some referred to them as 'Iron Horses', or 'the spaceship of the day', or a 'mechanical racehorse'. No matter your opinion, it was agreed this new way of transporting goods and people heralded a bright future!

Sure, the trains on the Hatfield to St. Albans line weren't as majestic as the Mallard or the Flying Scotsman, but they were still awe inspiring. The sheer size of each engine wheel was bigger than the average man and the engine cab had to be physically climbed into! Those facts alone were almost unthinkable.

Usually steam engines were named after famous people or members of Royalty, but Mike simply referred to the Nast Hyde vision as the Ghost Train.

Last night's reading up about the Royal Train had been eye opening: how interesting that Brunel was onboard the first Royal Train. It was, of course, entirely feasible Brunel had ridden *this* branchline!

Many argue that without the pioneering engineer there would be no railways, as he also created the broad gauge rail at 7ft ¼ inch, meaning faster and smoother journeys. Brunel was considered a radical: suggesting the necessity of a bespoke gauge for bespoke locomotives.

Opposing this, his friend-turned-foe George Stephenson favoured 4ft 8½ inch, referred to as the standard gauge. Despite Brunel's side of this particular argument, Stephenson's gauge was built on most railways in the coming decades.

He sounded like a fiery character, Mike thought to himself. On the subject of fire, and remembering the dangers of steam engines, suddenly a great thought for an authentic addition for the Halt presented itself - the old red sand fire buckets, nowadays considered antique. Decorating three such buckets with the initials HSR to represent the name of the branch line - Hatfield and St. Albans Railway - would be perfect. Mike smiled to think that everything was tying in well.

Brunel and Stephenson weren't the only historical figures every railway should pay homage to, Nigel Gresley's name should have reached the same level of recognition, but for some reason didn't.

Sir Herbert Nigel Gresley CBE was one of the most famous steam locomotive engineers, building the super locomotive. His famous first two engines - not just one but two! - were record breakers.

The Mallard even today holds the record for the fastest steam locomotive worldwide at 126mph. Flying Scotsman was the first to officially reach 100mph *and* undertake the non-stop journey from London Kings Cross to Edinburgh Waverley in 8 ¼ hours. In order to do this, the corridor tender had also to be invented to enable crews to swap over during the journey, as it was too long for a single crew to handle the train.

It caught Mike's interest to read that during the 1930s Sir Nigel Gresley lived at Salisbury Hall in Hertfordshire, near St. Albans. Did that mean this wise and famous man travelled through Nast Hyde during his local residency? The answer most probably was yes. It was a staggering thought!

Most of the land around Ellenbrook and Nast Hyde had been bought by De Havilland in the 1930s. During the Second World War, the Mosquito fighter bomber was made in its Airplane factories, which put the town on the map.

Workers travelling by train alighted at Nast Hyde Halt before the nearer Lemsford Road Halt was built, so as to hopefully keep the location undetected by the enemy in wartime. For the same reason, there also was no mention of the station on timetables, nor was it staffed regularly. An exclusive 'workers ticket' at a reduced price encouraged rail over road travel.

Developers bought the 400 acre site in more recent times, with part of it becoming the Hatfield Business Development. Hertfordshire University was also built on the plot; this was what the town was now known for. Ellenbrook Fields provided a green belt as a welcome gap between Hatfield and St Albans.

Mike found the local history fascinating - and wondered then about producing a simple guide book featuring the history of the old branchline to raise awareness, and perhaps aid funding for the restoration.

Chapter 20

One curious passerby stopped to ask Mike an unusual question, which rather threw him as he expected the usual query. Ordinarily people asked him either how it was going or what was he doing, depending on whether or not they had known about the project before coming across it that day.

"Had there been any derailments at the Halt over the years?" The man asked him. "It was common to have steam engines come off the rails, or so I have read."

Thinking back, Mike could recall only one. Now that he thought of it, when he'd been going through the accident listings on the country's railways, there hadn't been a note of this particular one. He supposed it was because nobody had been hurt or killed. As the man had said himself, it had seemed to be quite commonplace. Further reading from the era had shown lots of derailments, almost to the point that it was such a regular occurrence that people shrugged off the incidents!

"The one that I know of was a minor derailment down the line at the Salvation Army Halt. That was back in 1955, due to track vandalism." Mike added.

The man nodded and asked another unique question, but thankfully Mike was able to answer it.

He left after asking a few more questions about the history of the line - and having ordered a copy of the book Mike had not long ago finished writing.

'A journey STEAMING INTO THE PAST with Mike Izzard, The Hatfield & St. Albans Railway' was an apt but long title for his guide book. Along with being an aid to anyone who wanted to know more about the old branch line, Mike hoped it would also boost future funds for the restoration project.

**

In spite of the fact he could 'talk railways' for hours, Mike's preferred subject was wildlife, always pleased to see his bird loving friends stopping by for a quick chat.

Over the last few weeks, Mike had been paying particular attention to a fledgling baby pigeon born at the Halt. He had even gone as far as to name him Percy. Watching the pigeon chick copy his parents' foraging now that he could eat by himself - Mike was sure Percy was a male - he kept still so as not to disturb the lesson.

Of course Mike kept the bird feeders full, even though they were frequently emptied by the Halt's residents, and not just by birds! But even wild birds need to learn how to forage.

Arguments were ongoing that too many people put up bird feeders, meaning wild birds didn't learn to find their own food, missing out on natural dietary requirements etc. What a load of rubbish, Mike thought to himself. Anyone with regular feathered visitors in their garden knows they only go to the feeders when they want or need to. There was a lengthy gap between late summer and early autumn where there was a definite lull in feeder activity at the Halt, so Mike knew this to be a fact.

The pigeon population couldn't visit the bird feeders as they were too big for the inbuilt perches, but hoovered underneath as smaller birds snatched at the provided food, gobbling up any seeds that fell to the ground in escape.

Mike was delighted to see his pigeon friend, Alec, out for one of his walks. After exchanging pleasantries and discussing Percy - Alec had also seen the fledgling around - he asked Mike how his plans were going, complimenting him on the appearance of the old Ghost Station. No matter how many times he heard the term, it always made him smile - it simply referred to an old and unused railway station, nothing to do with it being haunted. Mike thanked him, and they shared a knowing smile.

"Recently I put up nesting boxes in the trees." Mike gestured to several.

"A great idea." Alec looked around them, spying the tiny wooden lodgings high above their heads. "Just as well you have a head for heights!"

Mike shrugged. "They needed to be high up to be safe. Nests au natural are at altitude." He joked. "I know not every bird needs that sort of help, but it doesn't do any harm to offer suitable alternative accommodation. I'm glad there aren't any cuckoos around, how awful it must be for other birds when their nests are stolen!"

Alec nodded in agreement. "Cheeky buggers. They are the squatters of the bird world."

Both men laughed.

"I've been doing more research." Mike began. "It is said that pigeons can be seen in flocks of up to twenty to thirty birds, they mate for life. I've never seen such a huge flock, the most I've seen is maybe four together. How about you?"

"I have to agree. It is uncommon to see baby pigeons until they are almost fully grown, our Percy is an exception." Alec paused as Mike nodded; he'd known this already.

"I learned something else - I didn't know that pigeons can differentiate between letters of the alphabet."

"They can really do that?" Alec gasped.

"Really." Mike nodded. "Back to the subject of railways, can you imagine a trainload of pigeons on the move for racing?"

They both laughed.

"A whole train?" Alec queried.

"They didn't always put on a whole train specially for race meetings. The necessary extra coaches could be added to any train, as long as it is kept within the limit. There were Special Cattle Vans belonging to every railway with the specific purpose of transporting livestock. Sometimes even whole farms were moved by rail, not to mention circuses."

Alec chuckled. "That'd be one noisy train. Not that steam trains ever could be considered quiet." Lost in his memories, Alec's eyes glazed over. Coming back to the present, he smiled at Mike. "You really know your stuff, don't you? You are full of useful information."

"Most of it is not so useful!" There was a teasing twinkle in Mike's eye as he replied.

They both laughed.

"Here's something for your knowledge, did you know the dodo and pigeons are related?"

Mike's jaw dropped open. "Wow!"

Alec smiled. "The collective species of pigeons and doves, three hundred and eight to date, are referred to as columbiformes. DNA testing confirmed pigeons are closely related to the dodo!"

"Well, I'll be!" Mike shook his head in disbelief. "I thought the fact that they could also have a miniature automatic camera strapped to their chest was the most remarkable."

"It would have to be a *very* miniature camera!" Alec replied and they both laughed.

After a pause, Mike spoke the thoughts he'd had in his head for a while now. "Do they call you The Pigeon Man?" He spoke teasingly.

"Do they call you The Railway Man?" He retorted in the same tone of voice.

Mike laughed again.

He was almost sad to see Alec leave some ten or so minutes later, but whenever someone stopped to talk it always took time away from working! Depending on the task, Mike could usually continue doing something during a conversation, but it was polite to pay proper attention to the person talking to you.

Mostly, he was happy to be involved in any conversation that cropped up whilst he was working at the Halt, but people were respectful and either didn't stay too long or chose to make the stop a quick one if Mike continued with whatever task he was in the midst of.

It reflected how his job delivering the post had changed over the years - there was no longer any time to stop for a friendly chat over the garden fence. Mike sighed. It was no wonder people lamented about missing the Good Old Days. As a youngster, Mike couldn't agree with the older generation's moan, but now he could see it from a different perspective.

Chapter 21

Research led him to all sorts of different websites, but Mike stopped when he found the 'Haunted Hospitals' Facebook Group as an idea came to him.

When he had more time, he vowed to delve deeper into the stories behind Hill End - tales from the area's history would make great additions to his repertoire, he felt sure. The stop was known for being connected to the County's Mental Hospital, having first been created to deliver building supplies for the site, then latterly for staff and patients.

Returning to his original search for potential paranormal investigators to legitimise the otherworldly phenomena at the Halt, a surprising number of results show up. Engrossed for the next hour or so, Mike learned a lot from the various pages his search had directed him to.

From the list of signs that a place is haunted, as agreed by virtually every website he came across, Mike recognised several he regularly experienced. It reassured him that he *wasn't* imagining things!

Unknown strange smells; someone calling your name; electrics or lights flickering; sudden drops in temperature; unexplained apparitions and shadows that come to life; objects moving on their own; the feeling of being watched; unexplained whispers or footsteps; doors that slam shut when nobody else is there... and more. Orbs appearing in pictures that weren't caused by sun or bright lights, for example.

After reviewing their credentials, as Mike could imagine that there were lots of charlatans in this particular business, he found a partnership that he liked the look of. Reading more about the people involved, he saw they had the necessary shared interests in psychology and parapsychology, but each team member had a different background.

TERMINATION AT THE HALT, GHOST TRAIN MURDER MYSTERY

One had completed their parapsychology dissertation on individuals' experiences with apparitions, and using a phenomenological approach. Another had a general interest in quantum physics and how incorporating physics with psychical research could help, also studying demonology, dowsing rods and abilities, and divination tools.

The third, newer member of the team had studied spiritual development, and currently held diplomas in ghost hunting, mediumship, demonology and scientific theory for paranormal investigators. Mike stopped reading to check they all were real qualifications - they were!

Visiting their website explained what they did, including home cleansing to remove negative energy, clairvoyance and clairsentience - when they can see and feel spirits. Despite his initial scepticism, Mike was intrigued, especially when he learned that some ghostly hauntings are so intense they can make believers out of non-believers. That was truly powerful!

The most common pieces of equipment used by paranormal investigators include Spirit Boxes, REM Pods and a Digital Voice Recorder to pick up EVPs when 'on the job'. Most also rely upon EMF meters to pick up changes in electromagnetic fields, otherwise known as K2 meters; plus static cameras, laser grids and a SLS camera. So, if a power source was required for any or all of that, it could fit into one reasonably sized van, Mike assumed.

Probably a fair chunk of their visits were to properties, so issues with controlling lighting and having a power source didn't happen. It would be vastly different outside at places like Nast Hyde.

Reading the horrors some people experienced in their own homes, Mike stopped reading when he came to 'phantom mania', deciding he'd read enough! Putting the idea of getting in a team of paranormal investigators to the back of his mind, he decided that he believed in the Ghost Train and ghosts in general, and that was fine for him!

Chapter 22

DCI McFarlane refused to believe that Reg's file wasn't where he remembered it.

Checking everywhere for a third time - every cabinet and every drawer; even all of the desk accessories holding bundles of papers - he began to wonder if the file had been taken on purpose!

There had been times he'd joked about a local Bermuda triangle swallowing precious papers and objects in the station house. He cursed it now, left with hoping that the file would surface somewhere - and soon!

Several days later, he resigned himself to the fact that he may never see Reg's file again. Despite having perused it many times, he couldn't recall most of the details! Damn his fading memory.

Roping another Officer into helping him go through the rest of the Missing Persons' Records, they eventually cross-referenced every file, without luck. Every file on the computer and from his mammoth paperwork pile, that was. Sitting back, DCI McFarlane worked on the assumption that they'd reached a dead end - literally!

Assuming then that the skeleton was Reg, without the file that was all he could do, where did they go from here? After all, would identification greatly help piece together the story? The answer was no, he realised to his shock.

As an orphan Reg had no family, and his few friends were interviewed about his possible whereabouts around the time of his disappearance - by DCI McFarlane himself, albeit off the record. Not many people knew him, as he didn't cross paths with colleagues regularly because of working on the relief rota. Those who did know him said that he was kind, good natured, always willing to help and generous.

None of his friends or colleagues would have had a reason to hold a grudge against him, never mind having any motive to kill him.

Likewise, none of them could think of a reasonable excuse for his sudden absence. Reg's disappearance caused a lot of concern amongst the railway fraternity. Putting the facts together pointed towards foul play.

Reg's hobbies, that they knew of, mostly related to the railway. There was nothing to indicate any potential suspects there either, but it had been a long time ago. Even if he did re-question everyone concerned, he'd guess that not many people would remember anything about the conscientious and private young man from 1971. Especially so if they had only met him a handful of times.

Concluding then that Reg's death may have been accidental, or a case of mistaken identity, McFarlane thought back to the surroundings in which the skeleton was discovered. He must remember to refer to it still as a skeleton, because he didn't have Reg's file to prove his theory either way.

He felt in his bones that this was Reg's final resting place, wincing at his turn of phrase. Nonetheless, the fact remained that nothing around the burial site had provided any clues. There was *not a single thing* to indicate what transpired!

Even after appealing for the public to come forward with any information, no matter how small or how unlikely they thought it might be connected.

Zip. Zilch. Nada.

There had been a few busybodies, as he liked to refer to them, who had given the police very imaginative suggestions. Some potential leads had shown promise in the earlier stages, to fall short not long into investigating.

If there had been a clue, even something slight, even something seemingly unconnected... But no. That was seemingly too much to ask for.

The few things that had been found at Nast Hyde since the discovery of the skeleton he had really wanted to be useful. However, there was no way that an old railway uniform button, a man's cufflink and some club's tarnished badge could help them. Perhaps the badge was something the railway collectors would be able to identify - but after an investigation into this, nothing showed up!

If this had been a TV episode, things would have been wrapped up neatly by now. To be fair, not every murder investigation was this complex.

McFarlane sighed. It was all so hopeless!

Chapter 23

To Mike's complete surprise, his efforts at restoring Nast Hyde Halt were nominated for an award. Invited to 'The Campus' in Welwyn Garden City for their Awards Night on Monday 23rd May 2016, he never dreamed he might actually win.

Intent on enjoying the evening no matter the outcome, Mike took in the other people present. One of his favourite pastimes was people watching. Throughout television history, detectives were able to tell a lot about a person solely by watching them and it was a commendable skill, but Mike also could do this. The old adage of 'never judge a book by its cover' rang true with Mike time and time again.

As the evening passed, neither going slowly or quickly, he had been surprised by how many people seemed to know who he was and about the work behind his Award nomination. Thinking that he had changed lives for the people of Ellenbrook and the surrounding area who used The Alban Way, he was amazed to learn that his project had spurred on others further afield. It had all sparked a pleasing domino effect, resulting in more areas that had previously been abandoned or fallen into disrepair being enthusiastically organised and rebuilt.

The Welwyn Hatfield Borough Council Civic Award for the renovation of the old station and surrounding area had been bestowed upon him! Mike's jaw dropped open in shock. He had to pinch himself to double check that this wasn't a dream.

The day was one that would remain with him for a very long time. Presented by Town Mayor and Councillor, Lynne Sparks, and the head of Serco, Phil Bragiotti, Mike smiled for many photos and questions asked of him in front of the large audience and several VIPs.

Giving a short 'thank you' speech, he proclaimed that he hadn't yet finished his work at Nast Hyde to rousing cheers.

**

Taking his ringing phone from his pocket, Mike smiled to see it was DCI McFarlane that was calling. He instantly wondered if the news was good or bad, because he'd heard nothing for a long time.

"DCI McFarlane, what a nice surprise. How are you?" Mike answered cheerfully.

"Not many people are happy to answer one of my calls, Mr Izzard."

Mike thought he detected a half joking tone to the DCI's voice. He started to say that it was impossible to arrest someone over the phone, but held his tongue.

"This is only a quick call." He continued. "We came up against so many unanswerable questions, it is impossible to solve the case."

"Oh!" Although he'd half expected it, the words took Mike's breath away.

McFarlane cleared his throat. "That is, I assume you have made no other important findings?" A note of hopefulness resounded in his voice.

Mike was almost disappointed that he had nothing to report. "No, I'm afraid not. Apart from the usual debris and fragments of Roman pottery, plus the button, cufflink and badge, of course. Did you get anything from the badge?"

"Alas, no. Nothing came of it. I agree with your thinking that it is an old club badge, possibly a membership token, but our sources failed to come up with any information." DCI McFarlane's voice was flat. "I expected you to say there was nothing else, but I had to ask. Thank you for your assistance throughout the case. If you do need any help from the police, you have it. I wish you well with your restoration plans - and congratulations on the Civic Award."

Mike could've sworn he heard the smile in the DCI's voice. "Thank you." He replied before they exchanged goodbyes.

**

In further recognition of his work that same year, Mike received a reward in the 'Community' category of the Hatfield Town Council Sports and Community Awards. The thought that the Halt was award winning gave him a great thrill!

Initially, he had started with the intention of cleaning up the site. He hadn't counted on falling in love with the local branch line history. Once the community had likewise fallen for him - encouraging him to continue the restoration, he simply couldn't give up at the point everyone else deemed was only half way.

Of all the ideas for appropriate signage he'd received, he agreed with them all. Those would be relatively easy to replicate, and a piece on the railway's history was suggested. Some sort of all-weather story board, much as you saw at nature sites, would work. There was a noticeboard already for the Ellenbrook community, and he could foresee using that for advertising future events.

His imagination was ignited...

Chapter 24

Mike's mind remained on the mystery badge he'd found along with the railway uniform button.

Having failed to identify it by online searching, Mike wasn't entirely convinced of *ever* getting the badge identified correctly, especially if the police couldn't find any information either.

The more he looked at it, the more he saw how damaged it was - although there were words, none could be clearly made out. However! If it did turn out to be a clue, he owed it to the police - and to the young man whose skeleton had been found - to get answers.

"In for a penny, in for a pound." He said to himself as he posted the best pictures of the badge to his social media page, with an appeal for anyone who knew any information about it to contact him.

The very next day, Mike was pleased to see he had several messages awaiting his attention.

Interestingly, several said the same thing - directing him to local little known historical society websites. The first site told the story of Hatfield's Order of the Elite: information on this society was scarce, largely because they were so secret.

A clear image of a society badge was shown on the next page. Every member of the group had one, it was the same size as the badge in Mike's hand. Peering closer, he judged that it looked to have the same sort of decoration to it, although it was hard to tell what the writing on the badge had originally stated. It *could* have read 'Order of the Elite' across the top half, but the enamel had worn and faded.

Then again, he knew it could be his overactive imagination telling him it was a definite match. But the responses he'd gleaned online had all pointed towards the badge being similar, if not a complete match, of those from the secret society.

Someone else had commented that most metal enamel badges tarnished over time, but that could be easily cleaned off - with the right materials. Researching it, Mike was amazed to learn that these types of badges had been made for a very long time, far longer than he'd thought, and the material could stand the test of time, in the right conditions.

Such little coloured badges, known as enamel pins, were responsible for some of the biggest movements and uprisings in modern history. They alone had the power to unite a divided nation, and equally sell 1 billion bottles of the most desired sugared pop commonly known as Coca-Cola. Mike smiled to see this, as he was more of a Pepsi fan, but he understood the importance of the information.

Going back to the society websites he'd been directed to, he mostly skimmed over the rest of the details therein, stopping only when his attention was drawn to the last statement. The secret society had disbanded towards the end of 1971, for reasons unknown, with many of its former members moving away from the area.

Mike's excitement rose - the timeline fitted with the age of the railway uniform button he'd found with the badge! Surely the two were connected!

Remembering then Roy and his Dad, who were relatives of Fred Field, he wondered about asking if they knew of the society, or if they could remember anything Fred may have known or said about it.

Once he had a response from Roy, whether it was positive or not, he was then going to present this new information to DCI McFarlane in person - it was far too important to do over the phone.

Chapter 25

After months of clearing and cleaning up the platform surface, Mike was ready for the next task. Buying the essentials - concrete and sand, fencing supplies and paint, this was the first bit of real shopping he'd done as part of the restoration process.

Originally, he'd assumed a lot of rebuilding of the old platform would be required before he could even set foot on it, but he was pleased to find the aged brickwork mostly held up! This allowed him more time to learn the essential skills that would be necessary in the forthcoming stages, in particular bricklaying.

Fencing had to be carefully considered and be of a complementary style. Such small seemingly unimportant details like this could make or break restoration projects, Mike knew. Equally his paint choice was another important detail, recalling a story he'd heard from years ago when farmers of Nast Hyde South and North demanded the station's waiting shed be painted green to blend into the scenery.

All fence posts had to be concreted into place so that they would be strong and sturdy. Plus, if he was to affix any posters or decorations to the fencing, it needed to be able to support the weight and still stand tall!

Safety was key, he knew. At the Halt's first fundraising event some time ago now, several people from another restoration group had lectured him on Health and Safety. Specifically, how he needed to ensure that nobody had an accident for which he could be blamed.

Mike had nodded and said thank you politely, commenting that he had attentively planned for the public to access the platform if they wished to do so. This was severely frowned upon; the group tried to dissuade him, stating that it was asking for trouble. Again he thanked them for their advice, mercifully catching the eye of someone he knew so that he could excuse himself.

Not only did he have to think of safety at all times, he had to protect his investments. It struck him that should he be able to get his hands on any old railway station props, they too needed to be cemented down - but that would ruin the effects. A compromise clearly had to be worked out.

**

Having hurried to the police station and waited impatiently for DCI McFarlane to appear once Mike asked for him in person, Mike was relieved to be taken straight to his office. Did the policeman see the excitement of the discovery in his face?

"Mr Izzard, it is a pleasure to see you again. How can I help?" McFarlane asked, bidding Mike to sit opposite him.

"It is *I* that can be of assistance to *you*." Mike emphasised, putting the badge carefully on the desk between them. "I discovered more information about this recently, and I'm convinced it's a real clue."

"Really?" DCI McFarlane was shocked. "We had researchers look into the badge without success." He frowned. "What is it that makes you think that you know better?"

Mike grinned again. "I didn't personally - but the Internet did." He took his phone from his pocket, already having pre-loaded with the website about Hatfield's Order of the Elite. "Look at this." He offered his phone to the DCI.

McFarlane shook his head. "Too small. Tell me the website address, and I'll put it in here." He turned to his computer on the desk, duly tapping in the information Mike relayed.

"That," Mike paused as the computer screen changed and the main page came up, showing a picture of the badge, "is a replica of our badge, wouldn't you say?"

He was barely able to contain his excitement as he watched the policeman check the details in the picture and the badge several times.

"Yes, I would say so, but..."

"Now, go to the History page." Mike cut him off. "Specifically, look at the date the society disbanded."

McFarlane's eyes widened.

"Members of the Order were known to have 'evil' views on the world, what if the young man we found fell foul of those views?"

The DCI caught his breath. Nodding slowly, the smile spread across his face. "I think you're onto something. I should keep this while we investigate further."

"Of course. Keep it as long as you need to. I did intend to find the person who lost it in order to return it to them, but of course if it *is* a clue, then it is evidence. I would like it back whenever possible though."

McFarlane smiled at him. "It will be returned to you, I give you my word."

Mike thanked him and they shook hands, both smiling.

Chapter 26

Typically, the better weather Mike anticipated for the months of May, June, July and August that year turned into the eleventh wettest ever summer.

Despite this, he continued fitting in work at Nast Hyde during his free time. As a postman for many years, Mike was so used to the rain he often joked he barely noticed it! Ever since the skeleton finding, he'd kept an extra eye out for any potential clues - especially in the wetter, wilder weather that tended to unearth hidden treasures.

Thus, Summer 2017 saw forty seven fence posts erected on and around the platform. Hours of ensuring each fence post was concreted straight and rock steady concluded the huge job. Looking around, Mike attempted to calculate how many bags of concrete he'd depleted. Actual numbers were immeasurable - exactly a hundred had been required for the fence posts, but then there had been others...

Other bagged material ferried back and forth in his trusty car were of bark chips. Choosing these to deck the platform worked in many ways: the area would be easily maintained and pieces wouldn't slide off either end of the platform. An additional benefit was that they fitted in well with the wildscaping of the area. Generously donated from a local tree surgeon, a mass amounting to five tonnes shockingly wasn't enough - another 60 bags were necessary to finish the job!

Mike remembered not to stand back to admire his work, not wanting to fall off the edge of the platform! Thinking of that brought him to the realisation that he needed some sort of barrier along the platform's front edge.

Hmm... Perhaps the right sort of hedge could fit the bill nicely, performing double duties of providing a natural barrier for protection and adding to the Halt's well-kept appearance.

Already he had planted what his research deemed the best plants for the area seasons ago. Pleased to see these had spread to the extent that no unrecognisable plants could be seen, and weeds were minimal, Mike had to agree that the research had been right.

As a result, wildlife in the area had boomed. This year, Ellenbrook residents had reported bird sightings of Buzzard, Pheasant, Skylark, Willow Warbler, Chiffchaff, Whitethroats, Blackcap, Swallows, House Martins, a Jay, several Chaffinches and a Red Kite circling nearby. Mike was exhilarated by the extensive list already making their home here.

**

Often if the nation was captivated by a sports event on primetime TV, Mike spent that time at Nast Hyde, enjoying the peace and quiet it afforded him.

Having already spent months taming the area - snipping, cutting, hacking, pruning and tidying - he had been successful at conquering nature, but the work wasn't over. It would never be fully over, as most of the tasks he faced were ongoing. Tedium never entered his thoughts, because he knew the old Ghost Station had to look absolutely perfect for his upcoming fundraising day that weekend.

He found himself repeating the eternal prayer of the British outside organiser to the Weather Gods - please may it stay dry for the duration of the event! Employing a similar schedule to that of previous events, a local band was booked to provide entertainment for the day's visitors.

The more time went on, the more people lent their ideas to the project. Mike had, perhaps naively he admitted, thought that people would get fed up with him and his project, but this didn't seem to be the case at all!

The restoration finishing line moved once more as Mike's brain burst with additional attainable objectives. Next steps in the restoration were literal, as he would build steps for both ends of the platform, allowing access.

Then he would tackle the task of replacing the platform's brickwork. If the Restoration Gods were listening, he asked for them to be kind...One or two hundred, maybe three hundred bricks max. *Please.*

Chapter 27

Mike's wish for traditional railway decor at the Halt was granted in 2018.

Finding a vintage trolley and milk churns on eBay from a London salvage yard at a decent price was a dream come true. Although they all needed A LOT of work, this didn't put Mike off - in fact, that was what drew his attention to the items in question. Their rough condition meant a lower price could be negotiated. The salvager wanted to sell and Mike wanted to buy, therefore reaching an agreement wasn't troublesome for either party involved.

An added bonus came along when Mike spied the old fake luggage box in the corner of the yard. Fortunately, he *just* about managed to squeeze everything into his car for the journey home. Glad for once he hadn't brought Harvey with him, not only might it have been dangerous but the return journey was filled with alarming rattly metallic noises! No way would he put his buddy through that sort of torment.

Renovating the items in his workspace at home throughout the month of February, the year was off to a great start for Mike and Nast Hyde. Getting an idea for designing Roger Taylor's initials on the fake luggage box, after all that was what they did to differentiate between people's things, it would also be a permanent thank you for his continual support. Mike grinned. Sometimes the simplest ideas were the best.

**

Fixing bars were concreted into place before the trolley was positioned first on the platform, then those awesome three silver milk churns. Trolley paintwork was red for a reason - it represented Royal Mail, an insider nod to Mike's job.

TERMINATION AT THE HALT, GHOST TRAIN MURDER MYSTERY

Again Mike had the thought that it was a great shame everything had to be anchored down to ensure it remained, with concrete rendering the vintage railway props immovable. In today's turbulent times, it was a must to protect valuable investments.

Tackling the sack barrow next, Mike was pleased that it had a local heritage (of sorts). There was a beautiful story behind it, which suited his purpose perfectly. As a retirement gift to a former railway porter at Luton Railway Station, it had sat abandoned in the family back garden for years after its owner passed away. Being put up for auction at the same time Mike was looking for one, it was Fate that the barrow was meant to be at Nast Hyde!

With the barrow standing upright on the platform and the fake luggage box positioned perfectly, it looked exactly like a 1950s scene when a traveller was awaiting their intended train. The props added so much to the Halt, he had to admit he hadn't known their full impact until they were in place. Truly, Mike was blown away by the effect.

Every single thing he added to the platform, be it props or fencing or plants, he always kept checking on how the brickwork was holding up. Nothing was the worse for wear because of the added elements he was relieved to see. Soon, it would be time to redo the platform's brickwork, but not just yet.

Using the same materials and design from the sign and information post, Mike created a replica of a traditional lamppost. The issue with a handmade bespoke piece like this was that the glass panels weren't readily available - but Mike had a plan.

A lovely lady he had known for a long time crafted beautiful stained glass window designs, and so he knew where to turn. Assuring him that she had the answer to his problem, she then informed him she would need a week or two to work on the solution. He still wasn't entirely sure if she was somehow doing the work herself or not, and certainly didn't want to offend her by asking.

Arriving to pick up the lens specially made for the lamppost on the day and time he was told, he was astonished to find she had created two identical pieces, in case one ever got broken. How thoughtful! Mike was touched by her gesture and relieved by her foresight, especially when he accidentally broke the first one during installation.

The notorious steps (as Mike thought of them when he was reminded of *that* conversation) leading up to the platform at both ends were completed by the end of April. Albeit this was one of the easier jobs on his still lengthy 'To Do' list, but he was still pleased to get it ticked off.

As planned, the steps were secured on level ground, measured carefully so as to provide a few equally wide steps for accessing the platform. The wooden fencing around the back of the platform was extended at an angle at either end of the platform to act as hand holds and increase safety.

For now, the final finishing touch was in the shape of the three vintage red fire buckets. Not only was it poignant to have them because the sight of sand filled fire buckets would have been regular in the olden days, it was also an apt reminder of the dangers posed by the steam trains.

It had interested Mike to learn that there were permanent way gangs in the peak of steam train travel, in particular The Cliff gang whose job was to cut back vegetation on the red sandstone cliffs shadowing the Exeter to Teignmouth and Newton Abbot coastal route.

With no easy access points for firefighters to get to the area should it ever become necessary, this was vital prevention action to avoid any stray sparks from passing steam engines triggering fires. Mike hadn't given that danger much thought, but it did make sense. Nobody, even with the best intentions, even when following the strictest of safety procedures, could stop sparks flying around.

TERMINATION AT THE HALT, GHOST TRAIN MURDER MYSTERY

Permanently attached to the back fencing with the initials H, S and R hand painted on them in sequence, for Hatfield and St. Albans Railway, the finished fire buckets were exemplary. Mike knew the simplicity of his chosen decor had paid off. It all looked *very* smart, if he did say so himself!

For the first time since starting the plan to undertake Nast Hyde Halt's restoration alone, he stopped to look around properly at what he had achieved. At that moment, birdsong rose around the Halt as if in a serenade, telling him all he needed to know - he had really and truly made a difference.

Many passersby delivered their congratulations all evening, stopping to admire the results of his hard work. Some even patted him on the back and told him to enjoy the fruits of his labours.

As the sun began to set over Nast Hyde at 20:22, Mike was treated to the reward of a beautiful colourful glow across the sky.

Chapter 28

So much for his prayers for a minimal number of replacement bricks!

It had taken weeks to sort out the damaged brickwork to determine how much was required to be replaced. Cleaning out the weeds, roots and other debris in the way also, he saw that plants tended to find the smallest spaces to grow into, and in the unlikeliest of places, with their roots able to stretch for what seemed like miles! Nonetheless, it was imperative that the surface was perfectly prepared before the new materials could be laid. Such a mammoth task was certainly one that he wanted to only do once!

Relieved to have the Town Council's special grant pay the whopping bill of £1,500 for the six hundred necessary new bricks, Mike turned his attention to the actual purchase. Stunned and confused by the choices on offer of bricks, he learned that seven different types existed - that was four more than he knew of.

Between Sun-dried Clay Bricks and Burnt Clay Bricks, there were also Concrete, Fly Ash, Sand Lime, Firebricks and Engineering Bricks to choose from. Burnt Clay Bricks were also named as the 'common brick' as it was the option preferred for most construction work. Mostly the options were categorised into three main classes of brick - facing, common and engineering.

Mike had an idea that Engineering Bricks were the option best for the platform renovation. A quick chat with the expert on hand at Wickes convinced him that he had chosen the correct one. With high compressive strength and low water absorption, they were more used because of their physical characteristics not their appearance, although they are available in a smooth red colour or blue. This was the choice traditionally used in civil engineering, and most suitable for jobs where strength and resistance to frost attack and water were important factors. Plus, they were the closest to the original bricks used when the replacement platform was built when the previous wooden materials were upgraded.

Agreeing on a delivery date when he was able to be there to supervise, Mike had another problem to solve - somewhere to safely store them. A pallet of six hundred Engineering Blue Bricks wasn't exactly small.

Having done due diligence of studying the relevant instructional videos and tutorials to learn the essentials of bricklaying, Mike thought through what needed to be done.

It wasn't only bricks that had to be purchased, he also needed enough bags of cement and sand for the mammoth task. Mixed to a ratio of 4 parts sand to 1 part cement, Mike calculated that this amounted to another one hundred and fifty bags for the platform rebuild.

Preparation had taken him *hours*, far more time than he'd anticipated if he was to be honest. But it was a vital thing to get right. The gaping brickwork in the old platform looked forlorn and sad, but Mike reassured anyone passing who commented that it wouldn't be like this long. At least, that was the theory!

His pigeon friend, Alec, came to his rescue regarding a location for safe storage of the bricks in the form of his cousin Laura, who lived in one of the nearby houses to Nast Hyde.

Both going to see her, Alec started the conversation as Mike hung back, enjoying the comfortable interaction of the cousins.

"You can have the delivery dropped off here." She waved at the grassy area of her front garden, making the offer even before they had finished speaking.

"That's very kind of you." Mike smiled at her, recognising her as one of his regular supporters. "I won't intrude on your beautiful garden." He promised, looking around at the blooming packed out flower beds and borders.

"I know you won't." She smiled at him.

"Also, once the pallet has gone, I'll pay for the damage to the grass. It will have to be re-turfed..."

She cut him off. "There's no need." Shrugging, she laughed. "It's only grass, Mike. It'll soon regrow."

Eyes twinkling mischievously, she went on to tell him that she needed no reward - her view of the vastly improved Halt was all the reward she needed.

Mike knew when he was beaten. The last thing he wanted was to insult her, planning instead to come up with another way to thank her for her generosity. The whole garden was covered by CCTV up to the 4ft fence around her property boundary. It was perfectly positioned, as he had perhaps ten or so steps between here and the platform.

Alec detailed that on the day before, he would come to temporarily remove part of the fencing for ease of access: Mike and Laura agreed.

"You took the words out of my mouth." She teased him. Looking at Mike again, she added, "and if you play your cards right, I might bring you cups of tea while you work."

"That would be lovely, but there's honestly no need. You have done more than enough." Mike replied.

Alec nudged Mike. "That's a privilege. I don't get a cuppa, and I'm family." He joked, dodging her pinch.

Laughing with them, Mike thanked them both again before leaving Laura and Alec to chat.

**

Learning as he went along, as he had throughout the whole project, Mike was soon managing to average laying fifty new bricks a day during his time at the Halt.

At this rate, it took no time at all for the platform brickwork to look as good as new. Adding the classic white painted platform line completed the task, and satisfaction filled Mike. Checking his handiwork, he then resealed the paint can and cleaned the brush.

TERMINATION AT THE HALT, GHOST TRAIN MURDER MYSTERY

Now it was a proper railway restoration!

Chapter 29

The autumnal months of that year would bring Mike great highs, but also the lowest of lows.

Halloween at the Halt was an idea that he'd had in the back of his mind for some years now. Planning to tell ghost stories to a crowd of Trick or Treaters, the thought struck him that perhaps it was good that he hadn't actually had Nast Hyde deemed haunted.

Expecting a fair crowd after advertising his event locally, Mike was astonished that two hundred people had shown up! Perhaps his fame was reaching beyond the local community.

After this, when he was asked to hold a fundraising event for the Ellenbrook Children's Play Area, not that far from the Halt, Mike was only too pleased to accept.

His dream job of being a postman in a perfect village had come true, and over time he had learned how important community was. It was the same at Nast Hyde and Ellenbrook - giving back to a community that had accepted, encouraged and supported him.

Using the formula that had worked for his previous fundraising ventures, Mike worked to raise a whopping £5000 for the local cause!

On their usual evening walk, Mike was lost in thought as he and Harvey took their favourite path.

He jerked from his reverie on the home straight when all of a sudden Harvey slowed right down. Harvey's demeanour seemed to match Mike's emotions - what was happening to him?! They both shared the same terror that moment.

Scooping him up into his arms, Mike carried Harvey the short distance home again. Unable to think of anything but the worst, Mike recalled the night of the storm when Harvey couldn't jump up onto the bed without help. His beloved buddy was getting old - fourteen dog years is virtually pensioner age for humans!

Unashamedly, Mike cried as he cuddled Harvey in close as he began whimpering. Berating himself for not seeing it sooner, had he therefore denied Harvey of something that may have helped him or at least delayed this pain?

The very idea that he may have added to his best friend's pain cut him to the quick. Mike's sleep was more than troubled. Everyone around him could see that Mike's mind was elsewhere from that day onwards. His smile wasn't as bright as usual. His words of wisdom weren't as freely given. He was still as hardworking as ever, but his usual fire had burned out.

Local children of the surrounding community often saw Harvey in a pushchair on walks with Mike from then onwards. Poor Harvey could barely mooch around the house, never mind enjoy walkies.

They had all grown to love Harvey like their own dog. As Mike knew time was running out for his canine companion, the children got to see Harvey for one last time - although they didn't know it. With all treatment options exhausted after months of trying anything and everything, Harvey's sand in the hourglass was fast running out.

Saying goodbye was almost as hard as the decision to put him to sleep, but in his breaking heart Mike knew it was the right thing. As he couldn't ease his best friend's pain, there was only one option remaining. Supporting Harvey's head in the palm of his hands as the vet made the necessary preparations in the background, Mike lowered himself level with the table to speak with Harvey for the last time. Whispering in his ear that he loved him and thanking him for being such a great best friend, they both locked eyes one last time. It was as if Harvey truly understood what Mike had said, nudging his head as a way of returning the compliment.

Part of Mike left forever as Harvey's eyes slowly closed and he slipped away without a fuss within his loving hold. Taking his buddy on a last journey then to the pet cremation centre, Mike could only hope that Harvey was now free from pain and enjoying his new life far away.

As much as he'd been affected by the realisation that he was losing his best friend months ago, he was a shadow of his usual self without Harvey. Even people who saw him infrequently noticed a difference in Mike. Behind his public brave face, he was devastated.

The longest week of his life later, Harvey's ashes returned home. Immediately Mike set up the instruction that Harvey's ashes were to be placed in his coffin so that they could, at an as yet undetermined time, be reunited.

All of the heartfelt condolences he received at the Halt and at work were lovely to hear, truly they were and he did appreciate them - but it ripped open the wounds of his broken heart every time.

Percy, his once baby pigeon, stayed close by most of the time Mike spent at the Halt. While it was true that animals detect human suffering and sorrow, Mike hadn't known it to extend to birds, but then Percy was not your average pigeon.

The thought made him smile, and he realised it was the first time in months that he had genuinely smiled.

Chapter 30

With Nast Hyde Halt standing proud once more in the sunshine and the rain, this was Britain after all, Mike took some well-deserved time away.

Not that the theme of his holiday veered far from the railways, opting to visit the beautiful Nene Valley Railway in the Peterborough area. His favourite relaxation destinations were Cornwall and the Isle of Wight, so this was a little different - and racked up less mileage!

Had Fate brought him here, Mike wondered as he reviewed the words he was almost unable to believe he'd heard. After nipping into the office to give praise for the heritage railway, he met a man who knew who both he was and, more importantly to Mike's mind, knew of his restoration project.

Track and Bridges Manager, Andy Stevens, was as excited about Nast Hyde Halt as Mike himself. Perplexed as to why this was, Mike grinned to discover Andy had lived and grown up in that very area! With the upcoming 50th anniversary of the branch line's closure, Andy was only too happy to help Mike achieve his dream come true for something really special at the Halt.

For a split second, Mike wondered about asking Andy if he had ever heard the Ghost Train whistle when he'd spent time at Nast Hyde... But this was neither the time nor the place. Thanking him again, he left the office to allow Andy to continue his work.

He knew his enthusiasm slipped while battling with Harvey against the inevitable, so Mike now threw himself into hard graft. For any heavy jobs he knew he'd need more manpower onboard - he also knew where to turn.

Months before, two of his Royal Mail colleagues had offered to lend their muscle to the project at any time it was required. It seemed like he had gone from 'the postman with the crazy project' to 'the spooky Station Master' and then to some sort of local hero! Personally, he thought that the real heroes of the world were the personnel of the emergency services. Happy to inspire people and be a role model both in the community and at work, Mike was still getting used to having praise heaped upon him if he were to be honest.

The time when he needed someone else's help had come - 30ft of railway track was being exclusively delivered to Nast Hyde Halt courtesy of Nene Valley Railway!

Where Roe Green Siding used to be before Nast Hyde Halt itself was built in 1910, Mike carried out essential prep for the track to be laid. This way the cycleway path would remain clear and the track would (hopefully) not be damaged when Mike was not in attendance!

Building a traditional buffer to signify the end of the track would be an authentic finishing touch, he thought, plus it would also give more meaning to the piece. Raking over the newly dug out ground and setting up a wooden frame around the measured area - remembering the old saying 'measure twice, cut once' - Mike soon had the area ready for the delivery of ballast.

It had been a great coup, (or a bit of luck if you thought of it that way instead), that quarry representatives were at Ellenbrook Community Playground to help with the renovations when Mike was. Sharing their knowledge of where he could obtain sleepers (the large heavy beams that support the rails of railway track) for the forthcoming track delivery, they also offered not only to donate the necessary 6 tonnes of ballast, but also to deliver it for free!

Arranging a timetable that suited everyone concerned, it was one thing less for Mike to think about on the planning side - and one more thing to think about with excitement. He grinned, reflecting it was all truly coming together now.

TERMINATION AT THE HALT, GHOST TRAIN MURDER MYSTERY

Feeling much like a child at Christmas as he watched the truck arrive, Mike laughed to think that without the guys to deliver it, he'd have needed a steam engine to haul the load into place!

After the load of ballast was evenly dispersed before being raked level, it struck Mike that the area looked rather like a shingle beach. This in turn gave him an idea... A great joke photo scene was set up where he was pictured relaxing back in a deckchair on 'the beach', complete of course with the obligatory seashore paraphernalia.

**

More proof that the old adage of 'If you don't ask, you don't get!' existed when Andy Stevens himself turned up with the track delivery.

Mike excitedly bounded over to him to welcome him back to Nast Hyde. As Andy gave him words of praise through his astonishment at the transformation, perhaps it was something he would get used to eventually.

Utilising muscle power with help from Mike and Nathan, his colleagues, the hefty railway sleepers were manoeuvred into place after some fine tuning. The bed of ballast he'd prepared perfectly allowed a smooth surface for the sleepers to 'sink' into. There wasn't much time to take a breather before the next colossal task. Now for the rails!

As he'd thought, this was turning into another publicity event showcasing him and his work at the old Halt. Not only were his family in attendance for the landmark occasion, but there were also three photographers! Mike had become used to frequent photos of the restoration process so having another set of lenses, or more, trained on him didn't make any difference to his attitude. He was still as determined as ever.

Giving the nod to the truck driver he watched, as everyone was, the rails being lifted into place. This helped immensely as no way could even the three of them lift the 30ft portions of iron rail any distance. Bolting each section of rail to an adjacent sleeper once ensuring everything was level, Mike was surprised by how quickly the time was going.

Hatfield Town Council Leader, Lenny Brandon, had been there to witness it all, having asked Mike to inform him of the day and time the Halt's extra special delivery was due to arrive on site. Agreeing to pose for photographs with Mike supposedly checking the level, although it was of course already done, made a good picture for the waiting trio of photographers.

All that was left was for Mike to thank everyone involved; his motto that 'team work made the dream work' fitted here nicely. He acknowledged that as much as he preferred to work alone, for many reasons, it was great to have a team to rely upon when he needed them.

Chapter 31

The railways played a huge part in the British tourism boom, because until then people didn't tend to travel far from the place they lived. Many spent their entire lives, from birth to death, within the same few miles. Inclination to travel the world was mightily frowned upon; any young person wistfully dreaming of such were told that this was something reserved for people of a higher social standing.

Therefore, it was considered exhilarating to be visiting new places far and wide by rail. Travellers could follow the landscape outside their window changing from towns to countryside, and perhaps back again, as it flashed by. At that time, the motor car wasn't as common an occurrence as it is now. Needless to say, transport by road was improving all the time, but nothing could match the thrill of taking trips by train.

This was in the back of Mike's mind as he considered final decorations for Nast Hyde. Every railway station had advertising posters for a variety of tourist destinations - and a station clock! With space very much at a premium, Mike affixed his latest online purchase of the perfect station clock to the largest tree near the platform. Everyone walking through the old Ghost Station would benefit from a time reminder, whether it be good or bad!

Bright eye-catching advertising posters showed the ingenuity of railway bosses across the country in encouraging people to use the train for pleasure trips, as well as commuting and business.

Successful illustrations publicised zoos, parks and attractions of all sizes, as well as country wide events on a par with Ascot and the Lord Mayor's Show in London. Picturesque holiday destinations including Wales, Scotland, Cornwall, Devon, The Lake District and others also were shown. Seaside destinations promoted stays promising tranquillity and promoted the benefits of fresh air, especially looked forward to by those whose existence was trapped in the smog of bustling towns and cities.

Any vintage advertisements he chose for the Halt simply *had* to include one from the variation telling passengers about travelling with their dog, perhaps one that highlighted taking man's best friend on your trip for free. The other publicity poster Mike knew was a must related to his dream location of Cornwall.

It seemed he wasn't alone in his love of Cornish life; this was justified by the fact that lots of people stopped at Nast Hyde purely because of his specially selected Penzance sign.

With less than a fortnight until the official Nast Hyde Halt Open Day of 22nd June, Mike faced a race against the clock to finish on time.

While some people worked best with a deadline to motivate them, some hate the pressure of a looming final time frame. Mike fell into neither of these categories - but there were a lot of people relying on everything being finalised by that date.

His perfectionist nature also told him that he needed to fulfil his duty to his supporters. After everything, he couldn't even bear to *think* about letting everyone down.

**

Super pleased to have his new friend Roger Taylor officially open the Halt, Mike grinned. It had been the best idea, far more fitting than asking a local dignitary to do the honours, in his opinion anyway.

Dedicating the project to his beloved best friend Harvey, he was drawn into the now usual round of photographs and handshakes before his thoughts could turn melodramatic. Amongst the large crowd that had turned out for the day, Mike saw many Town Councillors and the Mayor, remembering how nervous he'd been at his first such event.

However, this was no ordinary event for the dignitaries of Hatfield, as they had gathered with a surprise in store for Mike.

Bestowing upon him the official title of Station Master in recognition of his achievements at Nast Hyde, Mike was speechless. Seeing this only made his admirers cheer and clap louder.

Chapter 32

Mike felt honoured whenever ex-railway workers visited the Halt to relive their memories. Without exception, every one of them referred to the period as the best of their lives.

He was privileged to listen to many tales as he worked on essential maintenance of the area. Whenever they visited with a railway friend, the pleasure doubled: several regulars began to routinely meet at the Halt.

From his research, it was said that the perfect locomotive had over a hundred special features - creating such a contraption he could imagine would have given builders, managers and shed foremen nightmares! Putting the theory to the test whenever he could with any visiting ex-railway personnel, every one of them agreed, but sighed dreamily.

Talking with an ex-signalman one day, Mike learned that communications in those days were by telegraph and morse code. He joked that in some situations, messages could have been sent by a carrier pigeon, but the man disagreed and argued against the idea, obviously not open to the jest. Oh well, Mike knew that he couldn't win them all!

Later that day, he was asked what the station name meant. It was a question that had become frequently posed as people took in the old Halt in all its glory.

"It's simple really. 'Nast' is an old term used to describe where boats are moored and 'Hyde' relates to an area of land." He shrugged. "No hidden wonders there." He often smiled at the person who'd asked.

"Steam engines were usually named after members of the Royal Family and famous people." One man offered during their discussion.

Mike nodded. "Far easier to name them than to use numbers to differentiate between engines."

"At least the numbers were five digits long, that wasn't too much to ask people to remember." He countered. "When certain engines were sold to other companies and renumbered, that was when things got confusing."

"Yes." Mike nodded. "Like with Flying Scotsman, there were five registered numbers for the engine but 4472 was the more famous number."

The man's eyebrows shot up, almost into his hairline. "My dear fellow! It is true what they say, you are a mine of information."

"Thank you." Mike accepted the compliment without saying anything further.

**

One afternoon, Des and Les, two of his favourite patrons, paused in their reminiscence when they saw him shaking his head.

"You should write a book." Mike began.

Both retirees laughed.

"Seriously," Mike leant on his broom as he pondered the idea further. "It could be called Footplate Foibles."

They all shared a smile.

"The market is already saturated with such railway archives." Des began to argue.

Les added, "besides, we can't write a book!"

Mike smiled and replied. "There's at least one book in everyone." He wagged his forefinger at them tellingly. "You really should consider it."

"Writing a book is hard work!" Les declared, shaking his head.

"How do you know? Have you actually tried?" Des turned his attention to his friend.

"Well..." Les tailed off.

Smiling to himself, Mike left the old friends to their conversation, wondering if he had sparked something.

From various sources, Mike surmised most railway shenanigans seem to happen in locomotive sheds, sidings and signal boxes. None occurred in a stationmaster's office.

Back in the day, stationmasters ran a tight ship and ruled with an iron fist. In smaller communities, the stationmaster was the stalwart leader of his town, not just the railway station. Responsible for overseeing the local railway, they often worked alongside the area's railway police - a formidable combined force.

Born out of necessity, railway police roles were created as waiting for a local officer would frustrate the interests of justice. The combined British Transport Commission Police organisation was formed at the beginning of 1949 from the old railway police forces, the London Transport Police, canal police and several minor dock forces. Any new members of the British Transport Police were recruited and trained in the same way as a local police officer, thus giving them the same powers of a Constable.

Predominantly, official business conducted by railway police related to accidents: large scale occurrences would have them working alongside the regular emergency services. Even so, Mike thought that dealing with fatalities on the railway would be traumatic for everyone involved.

Whether or not they were myths and legends, stories of railway enthusiasts decapitated after leaning out of windows to make video recordings or take photographs during a journey were horrific. Common sense wasn't so common nowadays, but even back then *surely* people knew such acts were downright dangerous, not to mention stupid beyond words.

As far as he knew, the Hatfield to St. Albans branch line didn't have a known railway policeman based at Nast Hyde Halt. Certainly, Mike hadn't found records of any. With relations strong between Crossing Keeper Fred Field and DCI McFarlane, whatever ranking he held for the duration of Fred's tenancy, he supposed there was no need.

Thinking of Fred Field, Mike looked up again at the old Crossing Keepers Cottage. It had changed hands three times since Fred's day. The first new owners renamed the property Roe Green Cottage, because the railway no longer existed and they felt it was a pointless name.

On the same wavelength, the next owner felt it an absolute must to reinstate the cottage's original name of Crossing Keepers Cottage in admiration of the restoration work Mike had completed. Humbled by this, Mike was beyond astonished to learn the current owners' main reason for buying the property was because of him!

Chapter 33

Mike prided himself on being able to answer any question put to him about the old branch line. His general knowledge was rather wide spread, but the last conversation he'd had at Nast Hyde had completely bamboozled him.

Relating it as best he could, he was somewhat relieved that nobody else knew the information he hadn't. He didn't feel so stupid now! Reliving the discussion, he looked up the information online to check its accuracy.

"The last train through, in 1968, was a freight train?" The woman had begun.

He had nodded. "The train itself was a Class N7/1, hauling banana wagons." Testing to see how much his new visitor knew about the railways, he'd been blown away by how she had replied.

"Not many people know that the banana is a berry. In botany, a berry is a fleshy fruit[1] without a stone (referred to as a pit) produced from a single flower containing one ovary[2]. Berries defined in this way include grapes, currants and tomatoes, as well as cucumbers, eggplants (also called aubergines) and bananas, but exclude certain fruits given the culinary definition of berries, such as strawberries and raspberries.

True berries, or 'baccae', may also have a thin outer skin, not self-supporting when removed from the berry. Examples are the orange, kumquat and lemon: each is a berry with a thick rind and a segmented juicy interior. Drupes can be varyingly distinguished from botanical berries. These are fleshy fruits produced from a usually single-seeded ovary, with an endocarp (hard woody layer) surrounding the seed. Examples are the stone fruits of the genus *Prunus*, known to us as peaches, plums and cherries, olives, coconut and bayberry.

---

1.   https://en.m.wikipedia.org/wiki/Fruit

2.   https://en.m.wikipedia.org/wiki/Ovary_(botany)

Aggregate, or compound, fruits contain seeds from different ovaries of a single flower, with the individual "fruitlets" joining together upon maturity to form a complete fruit. Examples of aggregate fruits commonly called berries include members of the genus *Rubus*, such as the blackberry and raspberry. However, they aren't berries botanically."

Mike fought his temptation to respond by asking why they had the word 'berry' in the name of the fruit if it wasn't actually a berry. He also deliberated conversing about the toxicity of plants that his research had shone a light on, but he decided against it. Was this woman's profession a lecturer or a scientist? Certainly she spoke as if she was one or the other.

"Wow, I didn't know that." Deciding to play it safe, he responded neutrally.

Fortunately, such scholarly discussion wasn't a commonplace experience!

"Do you have music playing while you're here, y'know for the quiet times?" One youth asked during a stop off at the Halt on his way home from college.

Mike laughed, unable to help it. "There aren't any quiet times here!" Seeing the lad's face fall, he elaborated. "Listening to the sounds of nature around us is enough. You can't beat it."

"Who are your favourite groups?" The lad pressed. "Someone as cool as you must have great taste."

Fighting the urge to laugh again as Mike never once thought of himself as 'cool', he pondered his answer, deciding to be truthful. "You might not know him, my idol is Adam Ant."

"Nah, never heard of him." His admittance made Mike visibly wince. "But if you like him, he must be good. I'll look him up, thanks."

Stunned, Mike hardly knew what to say. Obviously he was more of an inspiration to the people of Hatfield than he'd dared to dream.

Other people passing by the Halt that day also had music on their minds, as Mike was drawn into several conversations centring around rail themed songs. He learned lots about the music history of their beloved transport, realising that of the mentioned examples he actually knew more of the songs than he thought he did once they were playing.

Admittedly, most of the songs were about the railroads in America and Canada as opposed to the British railways, but a train song was a train song in his book! Playing a number of the titles that he'd found interesting from an Internet list of a thousand railway related songs, his mind again was blown.

Smiling when he found 'Ghost Train' by Elvis Costello on the list, he made sure to check it out. There were several known songs called 'Ghost Train'; on the third attempt he found one by The Stranglers he thought most fitting. 'Waiting for the Ghost Train' by Madness also had interesting lyrics. Some were more than a little weird, edging towards horror. Only natural, he supposed, as the Ghost Train was touted as the scariest of British theme park rides.

Mike sat back, thinking. His brain presented a carousel (no pun intended!) of memories from the last four years. Nominated for not one, not two, but three awards was utterly mind blowing. Sure he was a man with a mission, but had his efforts *really* meant that much to others? He fancied the answer to that was an emphatic yes. The third award, of which he'd been a finalist - the Valiant Volunteer award by local newspaper, Welwyn Hatfield Times - had been the icing on the cake.

As he had done for years, he looked around for Harvey, wondering for a moment where his canine companion was - until reality caught up with him. Suddenly overwhelmed by mixed emotions, he sobbed.

Chapter 34

As the group of four men stopped and gasped at Nast Hyde's 30ft of real track, Mike stopped his work.

"It's much bigger than I thought!" The tallest of the group uttered.

One eyebrow raised, Mike went over to talk to them, judging whether or not he could make a funny remark before he spoke. Seeing they were staring in rapt fascination, he nodded to himself.

"That's a section of real track very kindly donated from the Nene Valley Railway." He began.

Excited and stunned noises arose from the group.

"Can we touch it?" The youngest one queried. He spoke as if he was frightened of the words.

"Lots of people do." Mike smiled at him. "We can't begin to imagine what it was like to have steam trains running through our stations, so this is the closest we can get."

All four men nodded, kneeling as one to touch the iron rails with both hands.

"If they could talk..." The stoutest man almost whispered.

"It's so... real!" The fourth man announced.

Thomas, Edward, Henry and Gordon were their names. Mike learned that they were all members of a London model railway club. The foursome had bonded upon discovering they all shared a name with a Thomas the Tank Engine character!

"Are you into modelling?" Edward, the stoutest man, asked him.

Mike shook his head. "I don't have much free time between working two jobs."

"Oh yes, that's right," Gordon smiled at him, "you're a postie!" He used the slang term.

Mike nodded at the youngest member of the group.

"We've come to walk The Alban Way." Thomas, the group leader and the tallest one, began.

Henry finished the statement. "We chose a Sunday in the hope of meeting more people at each of the old stations."

"But especially you!" Gordon added.

"Your restoration has inspired people all over the country to do what they can to rescue their own local unused and badly maintained sites. Not just old stations." Edward told Mike, watching as his eyes widened.

"All over the country?!" Mike repeated in shock.

The four men nodded.

Trying to digest this, he turned attention back to them - and their hobby. "It's Hornby, isn't it, that is the most popular model railway company?"

All four nodded eagerly.

"Hornby became a household name, and not only in Britain." Gordon started.

"Originally, the target market for Hornby train sets were young people, but with an explosion of popularity amongst retired railway workers, the company had a double audience. No matter their age, everyone wanted to have their own railway!" Henry enthused.

Nodding, Thomas proceeded to summarise early Hornby history. "Toy clockwork trains were introduced in 1920, and 'O' gauge was created to run them on. Because of their instant success, the company brought out additional engines and accessories. Their first electric train in 1925 was changed to work from a six volt DC source in 1929."

"Hornby Dublo came along almost a decade later, half the size of the 'O' gauge system. Production stopped during the Second World War naturally, but when both gauge systems reappeared post-war, there was no longer a clockwork range." Edward lectured. "After merging with rival Tri-ang Railways in the mid 60s, Hornby Dublo ceased production. Many changes came about because of the merger, however the Tri-ang Group disbanded and was sold in 1971, so from the following year was renamed Hornby Railways. Decisions to upgrade the specification of most of the range in order to appeal to adult enthusiasts were made. Such improvements included finer scale wheels, wire handrails on locomotives, better paint finish on model bodies and high-definition printing of logos."

"Wow," Mike said simply when Edward had stopped for breath. "That's a lot of change."

"There have been sixteen different logo designs over Hornby's one hundred year history." Henry agreed.

"More than six hundred and fifty current items are sold by Hornby, as they are now known." Thomas informed Mike.

"Did you know Hornby produced the first 'OO' gauge live steam locomotive twelve years ago?" Edward butted in.

"A model steam engine?" Mike repeated. "Really?"

"Really." The foursome replied in harmony.

"Sweet!" Mike grinned. "I'll have to look into it, if I ever get time to myself."

They all laughed at the statement. Mike allowed them to ask their many questions, relieved that he could give informative answers to all of the questions he faced.

"Before I let you continue your walk, can you clarify something for me?" Mike began.

"Of course, ask us anything." Gordon immediately replied. His three friends nodded eagerly.

"How did Hornby survive when everything went to computerised gaming?"

"They released the first Hornby Virtual Railway Simulation Game in 1996, with a second version four years later which was much more realistic. Players built a virtual model railway[1] layout in realistic scenes, with fixed track parts, rolling stock[2], scenery and buildings that are similar to a real life model railway[3]. Plus, users can control the trains

---

1.   https://en.wikipedia.org/wiki/Model_railway

2.   https://en.wikipedia.org/wiki/Rolling_stock

once the Virtual Railway is built. Every engine on the same track moves at once, and in the same speed and direction, much like a real-life model railway."

"That is pretty neat," Mike admitted.

"Some people say it is geeky, and maybe it is, but it isn't only geeks who like model railways. Rod Stewart, Jools Holland, Sandy Toksvig, Phil Collins, Tom Hanks, Elton John, Michael Jordan and Bruce Springsteen are a few celebrity devotees. There are many more." Thomas told him with a smile. "Perhaps one day you'll join the club."

"Perhaps," Mike replied, "when there are 36 hour days in an 8 day week."

They all laughed again.

---

3.   https://en.wikipedia.org/wiki/Model_railway

Chapter 35

Melting as he looked into the young pup's pooling dark eyes, Mike reconsidered his decision to not take on another dog so soon.

When the highly excitable black Labrador puppy had become too much of a handful for his adopted family, they were faced with the difficult decision to rehome him. Mike's cousin, Louise, was fortunately visiting her friends when this decision was reached. She was in the perfect position to solve the dilemma, speaking her thoughts aloud that she had a better idea. With one call to Mike, she wasn't surprised that he dropped everything to meet the small gathering now at Louise's house.

"Basil is 7 months old."

That was about all the information Mike took in, already enraptured by the hound. Equally, Basil's full attention was focused on Mike - instantly they bonded.

Shortening his given name to Baz, as that seemed to suit him much better, their partnership was made. Introducing his new buddy to what had been his and Harvey's regular walks, Baz soon met the Ellenbrook community.

On his initial visit to the Halt, Baz was lost in the sights and smells of the site. Mike stood back to let him explore alone, catching his gaze when Baz was finished checking out his new territory.

"Well, what do you think?" Mike asked.

Baz bounded back to him, enthusiastically licking his new human's face.

"That's a yes to being Nast Hyde's new Station Mascot then?" Mike laughed.

Letting out a yip that was half growl and half bark, Baz jumped back to look around, as if to say 'where did that come from?', stunned by the sudden noise. Mike laughed again, making a fuss over him.

They were interrupted not long later by Alec, his pigeon friend, who stopped on his afternoon walk to be introduced.

"Baz?" He repeated. "As in the railway cartoon dog from the 60s?"

Mike's frown gave his thoughts away. "I've not heard of any railway cartoon dog." He looked from Alec to Baz and then back to Alec. "His name is Basil, but I shortened it to Baz. It seems to suit him."

Alec smiled at him, nodding his agreement. "It does." He knelt to give lots of fuss to Baz, before getting up and looking at Mike once more. "It's nice to see you with a dog again."

Feeling the lump swell in his throat, Mike returned his smile. "It's nice to have a dog again." He managed. While he knew no animal could replace Harvey, Baz was already more than a capable substitute.

"Don't chase the birds here, especially not our favourite pigeon, Percy." Alec warned him. "It might be tempting, but it's never worth the effort, trust me."

Mike laughed at Baz's expression as he looked at Alec, almost as if he was taking in the advice being offered.

**

The next visitor to the Halt who stopped to pay Baz attention was a big Brunel fan.

Isobelle shared her birthday, April 9th, with the great man. She took great delight in telling Mike the story behind the Box Tunnel.

"Legend has it that the tunnel was deliberately aligned so that the rising sun shines all the way through it on Brunel's birthday. It's true, I've seen it myself."

"I know. I saw an episode of a police crime drama featuring it." Mike nodded. "Brunel was an amazing man. It's as if he was born in the wrong century as some of his achievements were that advanced!"

"Totally!" Isobelle agreed, her eyes wide with fascination. "He achieved many engineering firsts. Setting standards for a well-built railway, minimising curves and gradients, designing and building bridges and viaducts. Even the parts of society that hated the railways and wanted a tunnel on their land so that it couldn't be seen, Brunel helped grant their wish." Seeing Mike nodding, she continued. "Did you know he ordered locomotives to be built to his own specifications, and all but one - the North Star - were unsatisfactory?"

Mike continued to nod, feeling her enthusiasm was contagious. "When he proposed to extend the GWR to North America by building steam powered ships, nobody believed him."

"Stupid fools!" Isobelle hissed. "The three ships he created revolutionised naval engineering. In 1838 with 'SS Great Western', then 'SS Great Britain' in 1843, followed by 'SS Great Eastern' in 1859."

"I expect you know this, but the third ship was originally called 'Leviathan'. As in, a thing that is very large and powerful. Some people referred to it as a sea monster." He added.

Isobelle threw back her head and laughed loud. "That's typical of him!" Once she'd recovered, she continued on what was definitely her favourite theme. "He didn't only build railways and railway architecture, did you know?"

Mike's knowledge of Isambard Kingdom Brunel had been exhausted: he shook his head.

"Organiser and inspirer of the Crimean War nursing service, Florence Nightingale, was greatly helped by Brunel's design of a temporary prefabricated hospital after she'd pleaded for help from the British government.

Injured men contracted a variety of illnesses due to poor conditions in the original Scutari hospital she was based. In five months the team Brunel assembled with William Eassie had designed, built and shipped the pre-fabricated wood and canvas buildings named the Renkioi Hospital. They incorporated the necessities of hygiene: access to sanitation, ventilation, drainage and rudimentary temperature control. Apparently, it was recorded that Nightingale referred to them as 'magnificent huts.'" Isobelle paused. "Brunel also was credited with turning Swindon into one of the fastest growing towns in Europe by locating the Great Western Railway locomotive sheds there. Because of the need for housing for his workers, Brunel built hospitals, churches and housing estates in what is known nowadays as the 'Railway Village'. Better still, his addition of a Mechanics Institute, and hospitals and clinics for workers gave Aneurin Bevan the basis for creating the National Health Service." She beamed at Mike, who's mouth had dropped open. "His work doesn't get enough recognition, wouldn't you say?"

"I'll say!" He agreed. "I knew he was a very clever man, but I didn't know all that."

"No wonder they paid tribute to him by naming several locomotives after him." Isobelle nodded. "There are statues of him too."

"Life sized." Mike added, remembering having seen it on his travels through London. "It's in Paddington, isn't it?"

"*One* of them is, yes. There are several in London, and six in total. One in Swindon, naturally, another in Bristol and another at Neyland. Another resides at London's Embankment, with the final figure situated in the grounds of Brunel University, in Uxbridge."

Mike's eyebrows raised. "I didn't know that, or that there was a Brunel University."

"They have three divisions of study. The College of Business, Arts and Social Sciences; College of Health, Medicine and Life Sciences; and of course, College of Engineering, Design and Physical Sciences."

"Of course." Mike parroted, shaking his head. "I had no idea."

She took in his amazement, leaving not long later to allow him to carry on working. Her parting jest stayed with him for days.

"Maybe one day there'll be a Mike Izzard statue in Hatfield."

Chapter 36

Planting more daffodils beneath the platform and on the cycleway edge, Mike literally struck gold.

Uncovering several coins as he dug small holes for the bulbs, he identified them as being pre-decimal, much as had been found elsewhere on the site. Oh well, who needed a pot of gold anyway...*!*

Near to where the coins had surfaced, but further down, he felt something bigger. Whatever it was, it wasn't as hard as the metal of coins... and more shaped... Bemused, Mike pulled out a ladies purse. Amazingly it contained two bank cards, both of some age, and both embossed with the same name. Some of the lettering had worn off, but it could still be read - Ms Angela Dimond.

Mike's next thought was to track down the purse's rightful owner. Internet searching had identified the uniform button, so surely it could also find the lady in question. If he was to take it to the police station, they might not be able to reunite the item with the lady owner, as he suspected that this had been buried for quite some time now. Of course, if he failed in his quest, that was what he would do. But this was worth trying first.

Pocketing everything he found that afternoon - and digging around more than he actually needed to in case there was more hidden - Mike continued arranging the spring bulbs before cutting his time short to investigate the purse's owner. As he had a name, and using the locality in part of the description for his search, he soon found that Ms Dimond was still in the area. Facebook seemed to be the new version of the world's telephone directory, and he was able to contact her with ease.

With his notifications set to chime, Mike had half his attention on other things while awaiting a reply. He had simply written a message asking her to clarify the discovery without giving away too many details, to ensure he had found the right person.

Her surname was unusual, but there were others with the same name showing up in the search from different places all around the world. She could have moved and married in the amount of time that had elapsed - he supposed the purse could be thirty, or maybe even forty, years old!

He accepted the fact that there was a possibility he could be on a wild goose chase. It was a one in a million chance - finding the purse, then the owner and reuniting both. From the meagre contents of the purse, logic stated it had been lost or stolen before being discarded. The thought of reuniting the purse with its owner was one that filled his heart with joy. Furthermore, the lady would have closure from the incident all those years ago.

His thoughts were interrupted by the sound of a message notification. Hurriedly, he opened it and read the contents; his smile spreading widely across his face. Detailing his phone number in the reply message, he wasn't surprised to have a call from her within minutes.

Not only had the lady kept her surname but she also still lived locally, inviting Mike to her home that evening to tell the story! Over a cup of tea, Ms Dimond filled him in. On that fateful walk forty years ago to her mother's house not far from The Alban Way, her purse had been snatched by a masked mugger. Shaken but unharmed, the incident left her distrustful of the overgrown and almost secretive route.

Already looking at him in admiration, she was elated to hear about the restoration of Nast Hyde Halt, promising to visit the site soon. Developing into a regular visitor at the Halt, she amended her routine walks to incorporate The Alban Way as she used to all those years ago.

Mike's latest heroics became a local media sensation when it was brought to light in the community!

Chapter 37

Searching the local news of Hatfield online, as he had ever since leaving the town, Nigel's heart sank.

Seeing that Mike's one in a million find at Nast Hyde Halt had made the national news, Nigel hunted for more information as the black cloud hanging over him returned. Since his forced move from his hometown at the beginning of July in 1971, forty four years ago this year, he had been haunted by what had happened - and what his younger self had done. On that night, Nigel's crime had brought down the whole Order of the Elite society.

Part of the eternal black cloud hanging over him was a voice in his head telling him that he would receive his comeuppance. Karma caught up with everyone in the end, Nigel knew. Over time, he had several fits of guilty conscience that had almost brought him to confess. The more time passed, the longer he got away with his sin.

On occasion, Nigel heard words whispered in his ear - *Murderer! Killer! Devil!* Shuddering whenever this happened, he was always beyond relieved that nobody around him reacted. Did they travel on the wind, or were they only in his mind? Nightmares about the whole episode and having justice served against him, in varying forms, had plagued his sleep for decades.

Sometimes the dream placed him back at Nast Hyde Halt, and he was able to hear the old whistle of a steam train as it rushed towards him. The high pitched noise seemed to scream the now familiar allegations at him - *Murderer! Killer! Devil!* - wakening him often bathed in sweat and unable for several moments to tell what was fiction and what was reality.

Discovering that Mike had been relentless in his search for the purse's owner, Nigel knew then that it was very likely the mystery man's body had also been discovered. The burning question was had Mike also found the society badge lost that fateful night? It would give away

Nigel's identity, thanks to the meticulously kept records of the Order. From there, names of the other members of Hatfield's previously secret society would surface. That in itself would open a Pandora's box...

Forcing himself to keep hold of his senses, Nigel read on, knowing he needed to eliminate the badge from the police investigation. Reports stated that the police couldn't identify the Nast Hyde skeleton, and remained in the dark about the whole affair. Nigel took a few deep breaths, telling himself to think. As they had no information about the murder - it wasn't even mentioned that the skeleton was a murder victim, that was a huge relief - it was highly likely that they'd be hot on anything dug up from the area.

Further research was required before he could make any plans.

Journeying back to Hatfield, Nigel found not a lot had changed since he had left all those years ago.

Easily finding the newly renovated Nast Hyde Halt, he shuddered as memories mixed with his vivid nightmares cascaded over him. Standing in the shadows, he watched the passersby going about their business for a while until he saw a friendly face. Stopping the dog walker to ask if they knew when Mike would arrive that day, Nigel was aware that by not entering into basic conversation first, he sounded suspicious. Voicing his admiration for the project, he stated that he wished to meet the man behind it.

This, fortunately, sufficed. Smiling at him, the man informed Nigel that Mike would be around later in the afternoon. Returning his smile, Nigel thanked him before making his way back into town until the later rendezvous.

Chapter 38

That afternoon, Mike carefully placed his camera in one of the platform's planters, intent on capturing footage for a future video. When the mist rolled in as the forecast had predicted, Mike found himself wishing he could actively summon the Ghost Train as this made the perfect atmospheric weather.

His thoughts were interrupted by a man stepping out of the shadows.

"I hear you are behind all this," Nigel began.

Mike laughed, replying with a joke. "Seems I'm a legend in my own lifetime!"

Nigel gave him a tight lipped smile, choosing to cut straight to the point. "I understand that you found my badge."

"You worked for the HSR?"

Nigel was puzzled by the acronym. "The what?"

Alarm bells rang in Mike's mind. True, nobody knew if the old railway uniform button and the badge belonged to the same person. What he *did* know was that the owner of the badge wasn't someone to anger. Of course, he wasn't going to tip his hand by saying that the badge remained in DCI McFarlane's possession.

Paying closer attention to the stranger's appearance, Mike deduced the man was probably in his mid sixties. His slight build and average height told that he was relatively fit and healthy. Despite his local accent and the fact that he knew of the finds made at Nast Hyde Halt, Mike wasn't sure they'd met before. Dressed in dark clothing with no branding visible, he chose his clothing much in the same manner Mike himself did.

Aware he was being scrutinised, Nigel realised it was time to talk. "Years ago, I was working on the local farm when I lost that badge. It wasn't mine personally. It was loaned to me." He added quickly.

Mike raised one eyebrow. "Describe it to me." Seeing Nigel baulk, he continued. "You'd easily be able to do that if it was yours. I wouldn't give it to *anyone*. It could be valuable to its owner."

That was an understatement, Nigel's mind spat. Sweat beading on his upper lip, he reminded himself to stay calm. He nodded his agreement to Mike's statement.

"That's very sensible. The owner can describe all of the proper details." He forced his smile. "There is a crest in the middle, with lettering at the top in a semicircle, and a word below the crest. Or, at least, there was. It has been lost for so long you probably can't read any of the writing. It must have faded by now."

"It was in a terrible state when I dug it out of the mud," Mike acknowledged, "but it cleaned up well."

Nigel's eyes widened. How could it still be in good condition after all this time? There wasn't time to dwell on the matter, he had to get it back!

"It wasn't yours, you say?" Mike spoke carefully, still watching the stranger's face.

"I...well, you know how it is. Family history and all that." Nigel swallowed hard.

"Someone in your family was in The Order of the Elite?" Mike's interest piqued. "The badge is for an Apprentice member of the town's secret society. That's a very interesting family history you have." He smiled back at Nigel, testing his reaction.

Grimacing at Mike's use of the name of the society and the apprentice title, Nigel knew that his suspicions had been right - the badge was a vital clue to the murder!

"Yes, but I don't have a lot of information about it." Nigel spoke slowly, shrugging. "I'd hoped it would give me a clue about my family." Deciding to play the sympathy card to try to win Mike over, he continued. "My family was wiped out in a fire when I was a teenager. I was all alone." He took a forced deeper breath. "It might have something engraved into it, or contain something that makes sense to someone." He flashed Mike a fake hopeful smile. "I can't begin my research without it."

The two men eyed each other.

"I'm grateful that you found it and kept it safe." Nigel said into the silence after Mike hadn't moved or responded for several minutes.

"Hang on," Mike crossed his arms over his chest, "you said that you found the badge while doing your family history, yet now you say you haven't started. Which of those statements is a lie?" Mike narrowed his eyes.

Knowing the ruse was over, Nigel changed tactics. "Give me the badge and you won't get hurt!" He hissed, sliding the long knife from his coat sleeve.

Unsheathing it, the next moment he brandished it towards Mike, stepping closer.

Chapter 39

"Now, don't do anything stupid!" Mike warned. "An old badge isn't worth getting arrested over."

Reviewing their surroundings, Nigel gave Mike an evil grin. "There's nobody here to help you, never mind fetch the police. Give me what I want and I'll leave you alone."

With the stakes raised, Mike made sure to move around so that his hidden camera had the best view of proceedings, unsure of where this confrontation was headed.

"How do I know that you'll keep your word?" Mike challenged. "You have an advantage over me, I don't even know your name, never mind if your story is true."

Nigel half snorted, half laughed before his expression darkened. "I don't care what you think! Give me the badge *NOW*!"

As Nigel lunged, Mike attempted to knock the blade out of his attacker's hand. Mike's heart leapt, realising the stranger was much stronger than he had given him credit for. Deflecting the blow to his wrist, Nigel slashed out again wildly - slicing Mike's upper arm. Red hot pain shot through Mike's bicep; the shock of being hurt fleetingly paralysed him.

High pitched multiple screeching began in the trees, sounding louder as a blur of birds swooped down on Nigel in an attack formation. Mike was both astonished and horrified to see that bringing up the rear of the group was baby pigeon Percy!

Taking advantage of this when he saw his attacker was distracted by the bird bombardment, Mike was able to knock Nigel to the ground. Pinning him down, Mike knelt on his attacker's torso, kicking the knife well out of reach.

Hearing shouts from the direction of the police station, he knew the cavalry were coming to his aid. Half of him wasn't surprised, the commotion was bound to attract attention - and not only from residents in the nearby homes. But before then, Mike wanted answers. His initial shock had turned to anger, the emotion intensifying with every throb from the wound to his arm.

"No innocent person carries a knife like that! Who *are* you and what's the real story?" He demanded.

The fight drained out of Nigel seeing the surge of people heading towards them, including the police. This was it. The game was up.

He let it all out. "When I saw you found his body, I knew I'd finally be caught. I didn't mean to kill him... I buried him to hide what I'd done. He wasn't who I thought... His strange eyes follow me everywhere." He spoke somewhat dazedly.

Mike couldn't fathom what the man was gibbering on about, but was relieved to allow the police to take over. The very moment they restrained and handcuffed his attacker, a piercing whistle sounded in the distance... The Ghost Train!

As it steamed toward them, Mike swore he could read the identification number on the front of the engine beneath the light. Wondering... He turned to the assembled group, speculating that at least one person would react.

Nobody so much as batted an eyelid, except for the murderer: his eyes widened in horror, then he muttered something unintelligible. Collapsing then, he literally died of fright in front of the Ghost Train as it bore down on him.

It all happened in a matter of seconds.

An awkwardness filled the atmosphere as after the man was confirmed dead, everyone's attention turned to Mike for an explanation. They all had part of the story, having either seen for themselves or hearing how the stranger had accosted Mike before threatening him.

Summarising the evening's happenings as his injury was attended to, Mike informed one of the policemen where his hiding place for the camera was. Playing back the video confirmed Mike's story: he was beyond relieved the whole thing had recorded, murderer's confession included.

Reaching the last minute of footage where the Ghost Train appeared, Mike was only partly surprised it was not in sight. Shaking his head, he spoke his thoughts aloud.

"Termination at the Halt."

Chapter 40

DCI McFarlane arrived a week later at the Halt, timing his visit to coincide with Mike's schedule. Both men smiled in recognition of the other.

"I had hoped the injury would not keep you from your work." McFarlane almost joked, referring to the sling protecting Mike's injured arm.

Putting down the secateurs first and wiping his hand clean, Mike shook hands with the DCI enthusiastically, all using his good arm. "I can't do much. The blade severed a bicep tendon, which needed an urgent operation."

McFarlane grimaced.

"I was lucky it wasn't my head - and yes, it is as painful as it sounds." He added, seeing the DCI was waiting to ask a question.

"Indeed you were lucky." McFarlane agreed. "I am glad that you will recover. Is there someone to help while you are out of action?"

Mike nodded, watching as McFarlane took something small from his buttoned front pocket. "John looks after the place when I'm not around, so he has volunteered to help out more over the next few months."

"Good." He smiled. "I'd hate to see all this work go to waste."

Mike shuddered. "That would be a catastrophe!"

They shared a smile at his over-dramatic response.

"Thanks to your recording," McFarlane gave Mike's camera memory card back as he spoke, "we solved the impossible case."

Despite thinking he had made all the connections correctly, Mike was stunned by this announcement. He was surprised when McFarlane also gave him the badge.

"Returned to you as promised." McFarlane smiled at him. "I knew the victim personally. I'm relieved to finally know what happened, we have wondered for a very long time - forty four years, to be exact."

"You knew him? I'm so sorry." Mike immediately responded.

Nodding towards the Crossing Keepers Cottage, McFarlane told the tale of Reg being reported missing by Fred Field upon his return home from holiday. The distinctive feature of Reg's mismatched eyes had been lost when the body became the skeleton, but thanks to the murderer's jumbled confession, the final pieces of the puzzle came together.

It was the only case he'd been involved in that he hadn't been able to at least assist in finding the solution. But now, he was able to close the case successfully - against all odds.

Mike contemplated his next thought silently while McFarlane spoke - yes, it definitely felt right. Smiling, he retrieved the uniform button from his pocket before pressing both the button and badge into McFarlane's nearest hand.

"Not that they mean much," he trailed off, shrugging, "but you should keep these. I had a feeling they were valuable to someone."

They both shared a smile again.

DCI McFarlane looked around the restored Halt in awe for the first time. "You have achieved something sensational here." He shook his head in disbelief and wonderment. "When I first heard your plan, I wasn't sure any restoration would do it justice, but..." His voice trailed off.

Seeing the Ghost Trains warning sign, he turned back to Mike. "I did wonder." He said to himself under his breath before they locked eyes. McFarlane cleared his throat. "Just one thing. On the video, near the end of the recording, there is a strange whistling..."

Mike's mouth dropped open.

References

<u>Including but not limited to these websites</u>
Wikipedia & WikiHow
 Ellenbrook Area Residents Association
 OneKindPlanet Animal Education & Facts
 PCRC, MentalFloss
 Wildflower finder, Teleflora
 Learning Herbs, Medline Plus
 NHM, CEH and RSPB
 Disused Stations, EORailway
 Railway Station Cottages, Network Rail
 The Spruce Crafts, Freesound
 Police Magazine, tandfonline
 Ghoststop.com
 WordHippo & The Free Dictionary
 The British Button Society, KellyBadges & StudioDias
 <u>Including but not limited to these books</u>
Signal Box Coming Up, Sir! by Geoff Body & Bill Parker
Along Different Lines by Geoff Body & Bill Parker
The Galloping Sausage and other Train Curiosities by Geoff & Ian Body
 The *Railway Detective* series by Edward Marston

Thank You

A note to say thank you to Mike for sharing his story with me; for his hard work restoring the Halt and all of the sacrifices he made along the way.
Thank you also to the readers,
every book sold in 2022 gives a 50% donation to
Breast Cancer UK and the Pink Ribbon Foundation.
Most charities were badly hit by Covid and lack of funding for various reasons over the last few years,
and every little helps.
I have always treated others the way I would want to be treated myself, long before the 'Be Kind' campaign. Please keep spreading the love!

Books by Yvonne Marrs

YVONNE MARRS

Can't Buy Health 3
Can't Buy Health 4
Can't Buy Health 5
Can't Buy Health 6
Can't Buy Health 7
Can't Buy Health 8
Can't Buy Health 9
Putting The Visible Into So-Called Invisible Illnesses Through Poetry
Castiliano Vulgo - Discreet Language
(An Elizabethan Story)
Harbourtown Murder
Inexorable
Termination at the Halt

TERMINATION AT THE HALT, GHOST TRAIN MURDER MYSTERY

We hope you have enjoyed this book, please leave a review for Yvonne and Mike.

Milton Keynes UK
Ingram Content Group UK Ltd.
UKHW040741161123
432684UK00001B/83